Essex County Council

D0309292

OLD MOORHEN'S SHREDDED SPORRAN

Another tongue-in-cheek romp for our intrepid decrepit heroes

Lady Amanda Golightly and her housemate Hugo Cholmondeley-Crichton-Crump return from their visit to Scotland to find a letter informing them that Hugo's sister will be arriving the following day for a month's visit, which sours Lady A's mood as Tabitha constantly bullied her at school. Her manservant's announcement that he is now betrothed to Enid Tweedie, sort of friend and general gopher, has already unsettled her. If that wasn't enough, it appears that, while they were away, the security of Belchester Towers was breached and somebody is systematically killing off the staff! Enter Detective Inspector Moody and Detective Sergeant Glenister, and all hell breaks loose!

OLD MOORHEN'S SHREDDED SPORRAN

OLD MOORHEN'S SHREDDED SPORRAN

by

Andrea Frazer

Magna Large Print Books
Long Preston, North Yorkshire,
BD23 4ND, England.

British Library Cataloguing in Publication Data.

A catalogue record of this book is
available from the British Library

ISBN 978-0-7505-4424-5

First published in Great Britain 2014 by Accent Press Ltd.

Cover illustration by arrangement with Accent Press Ltd.

Published in Large Print 2017 by arrangement with
Accent Press

Magna Large Print is an imprint of Library Magna Books Ltd.

Printed and bound in Great Britain by
T.J. (International) Ltd., Cornwall, PL28 8RW

DRAMATIS PERSONAE

Lady Amanda Golightly –
owner of Belchester Towers
Hugo Cholmondley-Crichton-Crump –
an old friend who lives with her
Beauchamp – her butler-cum-general factotum
Enid Tweedie – fiancée of Beauchamp and friend
of Lady Amanda
Tabitha Cholmondley-Crichton-Crump –
Hugo's sister
Ludovic and Dominic – Tabitha's brown-spotted
Bengal kittens
Evergreen – head groundsman
Phyllida, Ethelred, and Poppy Draycott-Bayliss –
friends of Tabitha
Plumstead – Tabitha's manservant

A team of occasional indoor and outdoor workers, including:

Outdoor
Victor Mangel
Edgar Drake – Ed
Edmund Darke – Edds
Edward Darle – Eddie

Indoor
Florrie Searle
Edie Haire
Beryl Sylvester
Madge Moth

Police Personnel
Detective Inspector Moody – of the Belchester CID – a man who lives up to his name
Detective Sergeant Glenister – newly moved to plain clothes, also of the Belchester CID
Police Constable Baldwin
Police Constable Spouph – not quite as ridiculous as *his* name!

Chapter One

Monday

Beauchamp entered the drawing room with a tray of cocktails, his usual duty at this hour, but Lady Amanda was totally unaware of his presence until he spoke. 'I thought an Old Moorhen's Shredded Sporran might be in order, as we've managed to survive our Scottish trip without either being murdered, or dying of hypothermia,' he announced.

'Eh?' she queried – rather commonly, Hugo thought.

'Excellent idea, Beauchamp,' agreed Hugo, giving the butler an ingratiating reply, hoping to make up for his friend's lack of manners, an unusual occurrence indeed, for she was the very devil herself where manners were concerned.

Shaking her head like a dog emerging from water, she said, 'Sorry, Beauchamp, old man. I was lost in a dream for a moment there. What is it you've brought us tonight?'

'An Old Moorhen's Shredded Sporran,' he replied. He knew at once what she had been thinking about, and felt the blood flood up from his neck to his hairline. He had not long revealed the fact to her that he and her old friend, and sometimes too obliging slave, were betrothed, and would be married in the near future.

'Well, at least we're back from that uncivilised place in one piece,' she replied, referring to the castle where they had been staying, rather than the country itself.

Beauchamp coughed delicately into his hand, indistinctly muttering 'Beecham' into his hand as he did so. This was a long-running saga with his employer, she insisting on the French pronunciation of his name, and he insisting that she should use the English pronunciation.

As he was the illegitimate son of Lady Amanda's father, the situation was somewhat unusual. His French mother, ex-lady's maid to Lady A's mother, naturally pronounced her own name in the French way, but was so *très snob* about having given birth to the son of a genuine English 'milord' that she decided her son should have his surname pronounced in the English way to emphasize where he came from, regardless of on which side of the blanket this phenomenon had occurred. From such simple beginnings had the current disagreement on the name's pronunciation developed.

The man himself had been unable to sleep the previous night, it taking him five whole minutes to slip into the arms of Morpheus, and during this dead time, he had devised the game of 'Beecham Tennis'. The rules for this game were simple. Every time her ladyship addressed him as 'Beauchamp', he would find a pretext for correcting her, albeit in an underhand way. The first one to get to forty points won that particular game. At present, he saw the score as fifteen all.

This, however, was a mixed match, and at the

moment, he hadn't decided how many games and sets there should be to the match. He was not a fan of Wimbledon, and spent – or wasted, as he saw it – virtually no time watching the television. There was always something active to do, rather than just sitting in front of a box in a state of fugue, living life at second-hand.

This time it was he who was roused from a brown study by an exclamation from his employer, followed by the words, 'Good grief, Beauchamp; what do you put in these things?'

'It has eight ingredients, your ladyship. Should you wish to know the recipe, I should be delighted to enlighten you, if you would care to walk down to the kitchens sometime.'

Lady Amanda had already switched off, though, and returned to her private gloomy thoughts. Beauchamp took advantage of the situation, and coughed discreetly 'Beecham' into his hand, and thought, thirty-all.

It was Hugo who brought her back to the here-and-now by asking her if she really minded him having a relative to stay. She replied in a lack-lustre manner, 'I must be honest and say that I don't particularly like Tabitha; she was a bullying bitch at school and made my life a complete misery, but we're all grown-ups now, and she must have mellowed over the years.

'This is your home now, though, and you must treat it as such. Before you lived here, you'd never even have thought of telling her she couldn't visit you, and I don't expect you to turn her away and send her to a hotel now. She is welcome here; but if she starts misbehaving like she used to, I shall not hold my tongue. Is that clear?'

'Perfectly clear and reasonable. I say, thanks, old thing,' replied Hugo, having broached the subject and received what he considered to be a positive reaction.

At that moment, Lady A abandoned the subject of Tabitha's imminent arrival, and raised the thought that had been troubling her severely. 'What if Beauchamp buggers off to Enid's little house in Plague Alley, and just leaves me to get on with things here on my own? What shall I do without him? How will I manage? I'll – we'll – have to move into a bungalow somewhere in ghastly suburbia. I don't think I can face that. Oh, Hugo, what am I going to do? How am I going to manage without him?'

'I'm sure and certain he doesn't want to leave his position here. Why don't you have a discreet word with him and ask him if he would like quarters for the two of them in the Towers? It would be easy enough to create a cosy little apartment for them, and Enid could then be your official dogsbody – sorry, maid – and you could actually pay her for all the things she does for you.'

'Hugo, you're a genius. And then she could sell that little box of a house of hers, and they could have some nice outings and, maybe, with the proceeds, she could buy herself a new coat. That old one of hers is getting to be an absolute disgrace.'

She put down her glass and headed for the door, calling, 'Beauchamp! Beauchamp!' but for once, he didn't appear at her elbow and frighten seven shades of shit out of her.

She had just left the drawing room, unexpectedly en route for the domestic quarters, when a cry from that direction froze her in position, as if she were involved in one of those so long-ago games of musical statues, and the music had just stopped.

'Zut alors!' she heard, and even her heart was frozen. For all the French-ness of Beauchamp's early upbringing, she had never heard him utter a word of the Gallic language, and she was chilled by the experience, her own mind following the same track and coming up with an expletive, *'Sacre bleu!'* Whatever could have happened?

Trotting as fast as she could, considering her somewhat bulky construction, she called out in alarm, 'Beauchamp, Beauchamp, whatever is the matter? Beauchamp! Is everything all right, Beauchamp?'

She found the manservant furtively muttering 'Beecham' into a hand rolled as if to receive a cough, finishing with, 'Damn and blast, I've lost count of the score now.'

'What the devil's happened to so disarrange you?' she asked, in a breathless manner, her mind still caught up in French vocabulary.

'I was just getting out the plate to give it a polish before we use it tomorrow night for Miss Tabitha's arrival, when I discovered that we seem to have been victims of a robbery at Belchester Towers. It's gone; every last piece of it – not even a pepperette left carelcssly behind,' the man finished, having lost complete control of his syntax.

'What do you mean, gone? How can we have been robbed? Everything was left locked, wasn't it? No one else has keys except us four!

'There were plenty of members of staff around in the grounds, involved in the winter clear-up, for security not to be breached. They'd have seen off any shady characters.'

'Maybe, your ladyship, it was one of our paid helpers who was into a little helping him- or herself.'

'I find that very unlikely. We take up references on everyone, and no one's been here less than a year. Somehow, someone has got into the place, and I think it must have been done under cover of darkness, when no one was on duty. We didn't appoint any security staff; it's never been necessary in the past.'

'Well, it might be advisable, in the future, not to leave the place totally unattended again.' Beauchamp's face was white with shock. He could not believe someone had been riffling through his pantry in his absence, and he felt almost as if he'd been indecently assaulted, or at least had his underwear drawer disarranged by strange hands.

'Sit down, man, before you fall down.' Enid Tweedie had now arrived, having been attracted by the hoarse French curse, and recognising her fiancé's voice. 'Whatever has happened, to reduce you to a state like this?'

'We've been robbed, Enid. Someone's got in and stolen all the plate I wanted to buff up to use tomorrow evening. All the good stuff's gone.'

'You spoke that last phrase as if there's some not-so-good stuff around the place, somewhere.'

'Well, of course there is, woman. There's a load of old plate up in the attics that we stopped using when the household invested in the lot that's been taken.'

'Why can't you use that, then?' asked Enid pragmatically.

'Because it's old. Some of the plate has actually worn off, and some of the pieces have suffered disfiguring accidents and are dented.'

'And will that really be noticed, when it's all covered in food, the main light is candlelight, and all the diners are involved in earnest conversation, not having seen each other for several years?'

Beauchamp answered this last question with a short period of silence, and one of his old-fashioned looks, while Lady Amanda, not so trusting, was muttering, 'It's Tabitha. Of course she'll notice.' Clearing her throat as she came to a decision, the Lady of the House suddenly announced, 'Get thee to the attics, Beauchamp, and seek out the second-best plate. Cinderella shall go to the ball, although she'll have to put up with a used ballgown.'

She then executed an abrupt about-turn and beetled off to telephone the police to report the theft that had taken place in their absence. She only hoped they could get out to them today, so that the place was not swarming with representatives of law and order when Tabitha arrived on the morrow.

They couldn't, damn and blast it.

Meanwhile, Enid smirked in triumph while her *fiancé* left the room, discreetly coughing 'Beecham' into his hand more than once, to put him ahead on points, even if it was cheating.

Chapter Two

Tuesday

Lady Amanda's telephone conversation with the police station had been with the duty sergeant and had, therefore, been polite and civilised, the sergeant expressing genuine sympathy with her plight.

It was a different story the next day, when Detective Inspector Moody and the newly promoted Detective Sergeant Glenister turned up on her doorstep. 'Only the very best for the gentry,' announced Moody sarcastically, as she bade them enter.

'Good morning, Lady Amanda,' the sergeant greeted her, with a friendly smile. While Moody treated Lady Amanda and her cronies as enemies, Glenister had always got on with them well, and become a staunch ally, helping out when he could with snippets of otherwise unavailable information, thus aiding the enemy and undermining his superior.

Glenister had also been transferred to plain clothes, and looked as if he had just walked out of a fashion shoot for the trendy section of a buy-it-on-tick catalogue.

'As you may have noticed and will have to forgive,' began Moody in his lugubrious voice, 'I have not dressed up in my Sunday best for the occasion of visiting the local title.'

'I had noticed that Sgt Glenister was looking particularly sharp, while you are your usual rumpled self. Well, never mind; it shouldn't affect your ability to detect, should you have managed to develop one.'

Moody scowled at what felt like a slur, and shot a glower at his junior officer. How come his little witticism had fallen so flat? The woman obviously had no sense of humour. He'd waste no more of his gems on her.

She showed the two men into the morning room: so sunny at this time of day and, in fact, chosen for this particular reason to be the room it had become. The carpet was a shade of light blue, while the upholstery and curtains were a cheery butter yellow, adding much to its bright aspect.

'Do take a seat, gentlemen,' invited Lady A, although surveying Inspector Moody with a jaundiced eye as she uttered the last word. 'I shall summon my butler, who will be able to give you more information than I, the particular items stolen being more in his territory than mine.'

As she trotted out of the room, Moody commented, 'Stuck-up bitch!'

'Oh, that's unfair, sir. What did she say to warrant that?'

'It was the way that she looked at me, Sergeant; the way that she speared me with her eye.'

No sooner had he made this remark than there was a discreet knock on the door, and Beauchamp entered, his footsteps making no noise whatsoever on the fine quality carpeting.

A sliding, slopping noise behind him declared

that he had not arrived alone, and Hugo slithered in behind him in his slippers – after all, it was the morning, and in the morning, they used the morning room. In one hand he held a copy of the *Daily Telegraph,* in the other, his reading glasses. They could get on with things, as far as he was concerned; he wasn't going to have his routine disturbed for anyone.

As the second pair of men took their seats in the morning room, the doorbell rang, and the shrill voice of Enid Tweedie called out that she would see to it.

She eased open the huge front door slowly, to reveal a woman dressed in a leopard-print faux fur coat, and carrying two wicker baskets. Behind her stood a tall man in uniform, with a number of suitcases grouped round his feet.

'I wonder if you would be good enough to inform Mr Hugo Cholmondley-Crichton-Crump that his sister has arrived for her visit,' she intoned, in the most excruciatingly posh accent. If she spoke like that all the time, thought Enid, it would be enough to make the Queen sound common.

'Do come in,' she requested as gracefully as she could, 'and I'll take you to Mr Hugo. At this time of day he should be in the morning room with his paper. Perhaps your man would like to wait in the hall with the luggage, and I'll come back to give him instructions as to where to put your cases, and where to find his own quarters.'

Good grief! She'd brought a man with her, but no lady's maid. Surely she didn't allow the man to dress her for dinner? It seemed absolutely scandalous to Enid, until she remembered that it was Beauchamp who 'did' Lady Amanda's roots for her, in the appropriate shade of blonde, on a roughly six-weekly basis. Provided the man never saw her in anything less than a petticoat, it was acceptable, though only just.

She led off Tabitha Cholmondley-Crichton-Crump, for this is whom Enid correctly identified the lady as, although she had not been introduced on being greeted at the door, to the morning room, where she knocked, then entered with the new arrival.

A thundering noise from the staircase notified all that their hostess had heard the doorbell, but been unable to attend to answering it straight away. This was confirmed when a breathless figure with slightly dishevelled hair entered the room and said, 'Welcome, Tabitha,' puff, puff, 'dear.' 'How delightful it is,' puff, puff, 'to see you again after so,' puff, 'many years,' and approached at an exhausted waddle, a hand held out in greeting.

'Amanda, darling, no need to rush on my account,' smarmed Hugo's sister, taking the outstretched hand, and giving it a jolly good shaking – none of this Gallic, modern kissing for them; a handshake had been good enough for their forebears, and it was damned well good enough for them.

The two wicker baskets she had been carrying had been deposited on the floor, and they now, alarmingly, began to jiggle around, while alarming hissing and growling noises issued from within.

'Tabby?' queried Hugo, who had abandoned his

newspaper to rise and greet his sister. 'What on earth have you got in the baskets? It's not something that Beauchamp's going to have to knock on the head for dinner, is it?'

'You silly old owl, Hugs, of course it's not.'

Tabby? Hugs? Yuck! thought Lady A, mentally considering the siblings' pet names for each other – although a tabby is a cat, and so is she, so I suppose that, at least, is accurate.

'I must apologise for having to bring them along with me. They're a pair of brown-spotted Bengal kittens. I ordered them some time ago and, as the breeder wasn't far from here, I decided to come and pay you a visit, and pick them up on the way home.

'Unfortunately, fate intervened, and the daughter of the breeder went into labour very early, and has been carted off to hospital to bring forth her first baby prematurely. The breeder wanted to hasten to her side, but didn't want to leave her husband in charge of the cats if she still had a litter of kittens.

'I was actually going to pick mine up a couple of weeks later than the other purchasers, on my way home, but now had to pick them up four weeks earlier than I had intended, while the other owners only got them a fortnight early.'

'I've never heard of the breed,' declared Hugo.

'They seem very lively,' commented Lady Amanda.

'I do believe one of them has broken through the wicker,' observed Beauchamp, while Enid took refuge behind a sofa.

Neither detective moved a muscle.

'I think they'd appreciate being let out of their temporary captivity,' announced Tabitha, kneeling beside the basket and starting to undo leather buckles.

Lady Amanda tried to call out that she didn't feel this was a good idea in such a heavily populated room, but her warning was too late, as two tiny furry bodies shot out of their wicker cells.

Both seemed to want some sort of police protection. First out of the trap headed straight for Sgt Glenister, and made a mockery of his smart threads by pulling a number of them with his needle-sharp claws as he navigated his way up a trouser leg to his body.

His brother was more adventurous and devil-may-care, and merely gave a huge leap after a few careering steps across the floor. He landed, paws round the edges, right across Moody's face, looking remarkably like a furry octopus with a fifty per cent deficit in the limb department.

Beauchamp was quickest off the blocks, and ended up with a furry whirlwind in each hand, his arms outspread as far as they could reach. 'I think I'd better confine them somewhere where they can't do too much damage to life, limb or fabric,' he enunciated, a wary expression on his face, as he marched from the room and towards the laundry.

'They make wonderful pets once they settle down,' claimed Tabitha, but with a wobble of doubt in her voice. 'They're only six generations apart from the Asian leopard cat, you know?'

'That many, huh?' questioned Lady A, doubtfully. 'I trust you won't be staying the full month as planned? I'd have thought you'd want to get the little darlings settled down where they're actually going to live, instead of in a temporary residence.'

'We'll talk,' replied Tabitha, watching with fascination as Inspector Moody tried out his facial muscles to see if they all still worked. He had four groups of blood-enhanced pin-prick punctures round his features, where the tiny feline had clung on, on landing, to get a decent purchase.

DS Glenister gazed, with woe, at his Bengal-damaged trousers and shirt. He'd not be able to wear these two garments again for any activity but painting and decorating. They were ruined.

Lady Amanda made noises about any damage being covered by the household insurance, while Tabitha approached the two men to apologise for the unexpected ambush by her two new feline charges. As she reached them, Moody was moved to vent his spleen.

'You stupid woman! Whatever made you let them out in a room with so many strange people in it? I could have lost an eye when that hairy hooligan landed on me like that. You must be even further out of your mind than this lot, so I assume you must be a relative; they say lunacy runs in families.'

'I say, steady on,' chimed in Hugo. 'She's my sister, and I resent the implication that there is madness in the Cholmondley-Crichton-Crump family.'

'With a name like that, I don't see how you could doubt it.' Moody was in full charmless offensive. 'I think we should both consider suing for assault, and consult the dangerous animals act to see if such a breed of cat is mentioned.'

Beauchamp was observed to mutter something, but only Lady Amanda was close enough to hear. 'Just a lot of little pricks on another little prick.'

Of course, this set Lady A off with the giggles, as she couldn't have put it better herself, and then Enid wanted to know what she was laughing at. The only thing that put an end to the embarrassing probing was a duo of enormous crashes which issued from the direction of the laundry room, and a couple of animal howls of surprise and distress.

Seven figures hurtled down the corridor towards the laundry room, each of them fighting to reach it first. It was Lady Amanda and her killer elbows that won – she'd succeeded in getting the object of her desire in many a January sale because of these formidable weapons.

Without thought for the consequence, she flung open the door, and released the two prisoners once more, who headed, this time, up the flight of stairs which lay just down the hall.

'Bum!' she declared, as she watched their departing forms. 'Double bum! Whoops-a-daisy!'

'Manda! Now look what you've done!' cried Hugo crossly.

'My babies!' screeched Tabitha.

'And guess who's going to have to catch them?' asked Beauchamp of Enid, who nodded in understanding, deciding that her beau would have to wear gauntlets if he were going to undertake such a perilous task on a regular basis. He could never serve at table with scratched and punctured hands. It just wasn't on. Although he could always pretend he was a footman – they always wore gloves and Beauchamp already regularly wore his.

Closer inspection revealed that it was the large glass containers of washing powder and conditioner that had come to grief, being nowhere near full and, therefore, easy for such small – but determined – animals to move off a shelf.

A discreet cough from the corridor caught their attention, and all heads turned to see Miss Tabitha's chauffeur-cum-maid waiting patiently for directions and instructions.

Beauchamp left the group to deal with the man while Enid knelt to start clearing up the mess. The rest of the group dispersed, back in the direction of the morning room, to resume their so unexpectedly interrupted statement giving and taking.

As they were walking down the hall, Tabitha was heard to enquire, 'Are the police habitual visitors to your residence, Manda? They seem to know you all so well.'

When they had all been released from the rather uncomfortable situation of being interrogated by a hostile questioner and dispersed in various directions, Lady A was passing down the hallway again when she heard voices in the drawing room, and just happened to stop outside to check that her shoe-laces were securely fastened.

The door was not shut tight and, from inside, she could clearly hear Tabitha's voice. 'What on earth are you doing, living here, under that old trout's roof and thumb? I can't understand how you put up with her, Hugs.'

Hugo's voice suddenly rumbled in reply. 'When Manda first came across me, I was bed-bound in the most ghastly nursing home, with only basic care and rations, and nothing to do all day. She rescued me, took me under her own roof, took me to her doctor and a consultant, and she's been having my joints replaced ever since.

'I only get the best of care here. I'm warm and comfortable, and I've got company. I'm also more mobile than I've been for years. Nobody's been a friend to me like she has, and she leads a most adventurous life, which has livened up mine considerably. And she didn't have to do anything at all for me; we'd lost touch years ago, and only met again by coincidence.'

'Tommy-rot, Hugs. She's using you to make herself look good and to bolster her already enormous ego. You're just a pawn!'

Lady A decided that her shoes were, indeed, properly tied and moved on, glad that Hugo had stuck up for her, but she still didn't like his sister.

Chapter Three

Lady A, totally incapable of leaving sleeping dogs to lie, after all the feline fuss had died down for a while, fixed Enid with a gimlet eye and backed her into a corner to discuss after-nuptials accommodation.

'You're surely not considering both of you living in your little hovel in Plague Alley, are you? It's totally unsuitable for a couple of your calibre, and I had it in mind that I might construct suitable accommodation here at Belchester Towers.

'There are certainly plenty of spare rooms, and we could create some very acceptable and spacious quarters for you. Will you have a word with your other half?' She shuddered as she uttered this final cliché, but its use seemed necessary to get the right 'pally' approach – something she was certainly not used to.

Enid, startled beyond measure at this over-friendly approach, huddled in the corner she had been backed into with the expression of a rabbit startled by the headlights of a car, and unable to tear her gaze away from the terrifying expression of bonhomie on the aristocratic face.

Stuttering like a terrified schoolgirl, Enid promised to speak to her beloved, and expressed her gratitude at the generosity of Lady Amanda's offer.

'And you could be an official maid, and I could award you a salary for all the work you currently do for nothing.' This statement was so unexpected that Enid had to put out her hands to balance herself against the wall, to stop herself from sliding down to the floor in shock.

When the terrifyingly friendly figure – a bit like a crocodile that expresses a seemingly sincere desire to take you out for afternoon tea – had stumped off in search of Hugo, Enid fled to the domestic regions in search of Beauchamp and sanity.

The two policemen seemed to want to spend an interminable time in their inspection of Belchester Towers for clues as to who could have been responsible for the theft of the plate, Inspector Moody in particular, poking into every corner he could uncover, DS Glenister keeping a weather-eye out for the two wild cats, even though his garments were beyond salvation.

They even managed to blag themselves an invitation to afternoon tea, and were still on the premises when Beauchamp retired to construct the cocktails, this situation promoting a wicked smirk to his face.

Seeing this, Lady Amanda knew her Beauchamp well enough to translate his intention and, therefore, on coming across the two detectives, issued an invitation to cocktails, but pointed out that they would have to leave when the residents went in for dinner, as Beauchamp was unlikely to be able to stretch his menu to include another two diners.

Thus, Lady Amanda, Hugo, Miss Tabitha, DI Moody, DS Glenister and Enid Tweedie assembled in the drawing room at the cocktail hour, when Beauchamp entered the room with a full and varied tray, and a satisfied smile plastered all over his face.

'And what delights have you mixed and shaken up for us tonight, Beauchamp?' asked the hostess. 'I hope you didn't strain yourself,' she quipped.

'Only those cocktails that required it,' he replied with an acknowledging twinkle at her appropriate jest. Beauchamp put down his tray on the top of the credenza, delicately coughed 'Beecham' into his right hand to catch up, then began to circulate with his delights. To anyone who didn't know about 'Beecham Tennis,' this small abandonment of the tray would have meant nothing, but he had confided the rules to Enid, and she now began to giggle, inexplicably to all others present except the manservant.

He began his circulation of the room to distribute the varied cocktails, starting first with the legitimate guest, Miss Tabitha. 'This one is for you, Miss Tabitha,' he intoned, indicating a glass for Hugo's sister.

'And what's this one called?' she asked, genuinely curious.

'A Jug Wobbler, miss,' he informed her with a perfectly straight face. The woman was of a rather stout build, and smiles were covered with hands, right across the room. 'For you, your ladyship,' he announced, approaching Lady Amanda, 'a Hammer Horror, and for you, Mr Hugo,' he turned around to offer the tray to the permanent guest, 'a Lawnmower – there is so much groundwork going on at the moment that it seemed only polite to make some sort of reference to it with tonight's selection of cocktails.'

Next, he glided over to the two policemen, offering the tray first to the DI and pointed out his designated glass. 'A Crater Face for you, sir, and for your colleague,' these last few words were accompanied by a neat swivel, so that the tray was pointing in the right direction, a 'Laugh a Minute'.

Moody's face assumed a murderous expression and began to turn a shade of purple that would not have disgraced the vestments of a bishop, but he did not have the nerve to actually say something about this grave insult. He'd have to bide his time to get his own back.

Glenister, on the other hand, had difficulty in confining his mirth, and his first sip of his cocktail was very nearly sprayed over his incandescent colleague.

'And finally, for my lovely fiancée, a Heart Throb, and for myself, a Hell Frozen Over. Chin chin, everyone,' and he raised his glass.

Lady Amanda knew darned well that Beauchamp never chose a cocktail without some personal comment or judgement in mind, and decided to spend any dull periods during the meal sorting out the less obvious insults in his choice of pre-prandial beverages, but was immediately distracted by a squawked question from Tabitha.

'Is your man being incredibly personal and impertinent, or does he just not have a brain in his head?'

So, the Jug Wobbler had hit a home run, had it? 'Not an ounce of wit, Tabitha, nor a grain of intelligence. Just ignore him, whatever he's done.' It was the easiest way out of a very tricky explanation, and she took it gratefully. Beauchamp would understand her reasons.

'That had better be so, otherwise I shall insist on him being severely disciplined.' Tabitha wasn't, somehow, convinced.

'Oh, definitely so. Not an iota of guile in the man; you can take my word for it.' Hugo's sister or not, the woman had better shut up *tout de suite,* or she'd be getting a four-penny one, and maybe a punch up the bracket to go with it.

Shortly after this, the two policemen took their

leave of them, Moody still looking as if he had been gravely insulted as well as injured.

In timely fashion, Beauchamp requested that they all take their seats, which were clearly marked with little oblongs of ivory on which their names were beautifully inscribed in an impeccable copperplate hand. He was a man of many talents.

When they were seated, Beauchamp rose again and left the room. No one explained, and he returned a few minutes later wearing white gloves and bearing a somewhat battered soup tureen, continuing to serve those still seated, while Tabitha surveyed him with a puzzled face.

No one spoke; no one asked what was going on.

When all the bowls had been attended to, the manservant calmly removed his gloves and sat down at the only empty space left, and asked if Lady A wished to say grace.

Tabitha, who was on Lady A's left at the head of the table, leaned over and whispered, 'Do your staff usually eat with you?'

'Beauchamp is engaged to be married to the lady sitting next to him who, after they have been joined in holy matrimony, will be joining me as a maid. Until now she has been a friend and occasional helper, but they are so much part of the household that we shouldn't dream of dining without them.' She crossed her fingers under the table, as this had only recently, since this evening, in fact, become the case.

It was all part of the plan to persuade the couple to make their home in Belchester Towers, and she hoped that Enid didn't blow it by commenting on the novelty of the situation.

At that moment, the lady in question rose and excused herself, as she needed to powder her nose. 'Really, Enid, you know you should have gone before we were seated.'

'Sorry.'

'Well, be quick about it. I don't want food going cold or spoiling just because you've got a head like a sieve and a bladder the size of a walnut.'

Enid turned a sickly smile on her hostess; she opened the doors, then froze as solidly as had Lady A earlier, when Beauchamp had discovered the missing plate, as two miniature spotted furry missiles fired themselves into the room and headed straight for the table.

'Ludovic! Dominic!' screeched Tabitha, pulling her arms and hands close in to her body to protect herself, as the two Bengals leapt, then skidded down the two rows of soup bowls, splashing the diners willy-nilly. One of them came to a halt, half-in and half-out of the bread basket, where he commenced fighting the rolls. The other had luck on his side, and ended up smack in the middle of the butter, which he proceeded to lick with great enjoyment.

'Beauchamp, do something!' yelled Lady A in a very unladylike way. The manservant, pausing only to mutter 'Beecham' into a hand, made a grab for the two intruders, who were so engrossed in their new activities that they were easily caught.

'Did you not catch them earlier and put them somewhere for their own safety?' queried Tabitha, scandalised.

'Where would you suggest?' retorted Lady A acidly. 'Down the well, as in "Ding dong bell"?'

'Manda! How could you suggest such a thing?'
'I find it very easy, after a glance at Sergeant Glenister's trousers and shirt and Inspector Moody's poor cribbage board of a face.'
'And where is Plumstead?'
'More to the point, who is Plumstead?'
'My manservant, who accompanied me here.'
Enid answered from the doorway, where she was still immobile. 'He's being served in the kitchen, along with a couple of our staff who were on duty today. He's being well looked after.'
'But he's not good enough to dine with us?' Tabitha was beginning to get on Lady Amanda's nerves.
'He is neither a relative nor an acquaintance of many years' standing. What right does he have to dine with us? He is merely passing through, and as an unfamiliar domestic, he is dining in the kitchen along with the other faceless domestics who have put in a day's work here today.' That shut the woman up.
'Have you heard that the trial has been allotted a date now?' asked Hugo, in an attempt to diffuse the situation, and in reference to one of her friends who had, in the recent past, been arrested for murder: an incident that fed the gossip-mill for a long time, and was continuing to do so now, even several weeks after the event.
'Indeed!' agreed his landlady, with no need for further explanation. 'And I understand old Mad-As-A-Hattersley's conducting it,' she continued.
'Bound to get off without a stain on the old character, then,' concluded Hugo with complete confidence.

'Who are you talking about?' asked Tabitha, suddenly feeling rather left out.

'Friend of ours. But I don't think we ought to discuss that at table. Rather distressing, yer know. Change the subject Hugo, and think of something nice to talk about.'

Beauchamp's return drew all their attention, and his mistress looked a question at him. 'In the old telephone booth,' he replied, supplying the relevant information about the Bengals' current whereabouts, 'For now!' appearing afterwards, to cough delicately into one hand.

At the end of the meal, he rose from the table and approached the double-length sideboard for the spirits, only to pull up a few paces short and exclaim, with horror, 'Not again!'

'What is it, Beauchamp? Whatever is it that's happened again and produced such a fearful reaction from you?' Beauchamp was usually imperturbable, and this was as unprecedented as his Gallic cry of distress earlier on.

Beauchamp, abandoning his game of 'Beecham Tennis' for the time being, after such a shock to his system, had to muster all his strength to announce, in a strangled voice, 'It would appear that the tantalus has been stolen.'

A tremendous breaking noise from the hall and the delicate galloping of tiny paws on the staircase drew their attention through the open door, and Beauchamp's temporary paralysis was broken, as was that of his partner. The Bengals were evidently out of the old telephone booth and on the loose again.

'That sounded just like my Japanese vase,'

declared Lady A with tremendous powers of clairvoyance, as she rose from the table to confirm her prediction.

'That sounded like them going upstairs again. Dear God! I do believe that, just this once, I left my room door open,' fussed Hugo, while visions of shredded winter drawers danced in his head.

A loud metallic boom, followed by what sounded like the landing of shrapnel at the scene of the incident, now echoed through the hall, and a posse of concerned elderly people exited the dining room and headed for the stairs, watched by a trio of heads round the kitchen door frame, one of which belonged to Plumstead.

On the landing, a collection of metal objects was still rocking gently on the floor, while in the midst of them, lay a suit of armour, once proudly upstanding in the corner to the rear of the space.

'Dear God! They can't have had something that heavy over, can they?'

'They're very strong, you know,' Tabitha defended the breed, 'And fearfully intelligent. If there was any way of getting that thing over, they'd have worked it out. They're fast thinkers, too. It must have been set up wonky.'

'Bully for them! Have you any idea how much it costs per hour for the services of an armourer, these days? And it was perfectly set-up before.'

'Of course I haven't, Manda. Surely you don't think I live in a mausoleum similar to this, do you?'

'That's Lady Amanda to you, Tabitha,' replied the lady of the house, becoming haughty and distant. This, on top of the Japanese vase was not going to prove easy to forgive, and expensive to put right, too.

'What is that dreadful smell?!' Hugo was always the pragmatic one, and he'd been wondering, since they'd arrived on the landing, what the rather nefarious niff that had been assaulting his nostrils was.

Enid was definitely the one who screamed first, and who announced, 'There's someone in that suit of armour. There's a body in it!'

And after Beauchamp had switched on the light and they had all looked a little more carefully, they realised that she was absolutely right, and the smell wafting around them declared that it was not a very fresh one, either.

'Someone's definitely been mucking about with my armour,' declared its owner. 'That's why it was easy to dislodge. It must have been left at an angle. Sheeh! That does smell rank.'

Manda, Hugo, and Tabitha had retired, in a state of shock, to the drawing room, where Beauchamp served them with coffee, and DI Moody summoned a Scene of Crime Unit and the Forensic Medical Examiner. He was in his element, now, what with there having been two burglaries – one must not forget the tantalus – and a murder at the (stately) home of his arch-enemy.

That part of the house had been awash with cameramen, both still and moving, men dusting for fingerprints and other miscellaneous bodies, all concerned with the particular one that had unexpectedly turned up in the suit of armour. Thus, those staying on the premises decided to have an early night and leave them all to their various specialist tasks. Beauchamp could lock up after them when they left.

No further news reached the occupants of Belchester Towers that evening.

Chapter Four

Wednesday

Not a word about the finding of a corpse inside an ancient suit of armour was said at breakfast, all the diners being much too nice-mouthed to discuss something so distasteful while they were at table.

Gossip had been rife in the kitchen before the meal was served, however, although it was accompanied by a most un-human yowling. Beauchamp had suddenly remembered that, years ago, when the family had had several miniature Dachshunds, his lordship had had a large metal cage constructed out of a stout mesh, for when they got too playful and annoyingly underfoot.

This, he had remembered, also, had been stored in the barn when the last of them had gone to that great kennel in the sky, and he had retrieved it, got a couple of the outside staff engaged on the winter tidy-up to clean it, and installed it in a dead space in the kitchen. With the little devils in that stout place of confinement, it might be a little less peaceful in the domestic quarters, but at least they knew where the hairy devils were every minute of the day and there would be no more feline mayhem to deal with.

About ten o'clock, the two plain-clothes policemen appeared again on the front steps, DS Glenister looking his usual amiable self, DI Moody like a man on a mission. He'd get one over on that uppity old witch this time, or he was a Chinaman.

Maybe she was hard up, and had arranged to fence all the plate and that tantalising thingumajig, then knocked off the man she'd hired to do it, and hidden his body in that suit of armour? As far as he was concerned, that was as good a theory as any, and one that filled his very soul with the deepest satisfaction; that, and the thought that he'd get to lock Lady Muck up for a good many years.

At their arrival, Hugo made a, for him, sudden decision to ask Tabitha if she'd like to go out for a ride on the tricycles. It was brisk weather, but they could just nip into Belchester and have a nice cup of hot chocolate.

His sister was intrigued at the idea of riding a tricycle, which was something she had never done before, and agreed eagerly, especially when she'd just caught sight of that grim man with the punctured face who had so blighted cocktails the night before. The younger one was OK, but the older detective looked like he specialised in terrorising innocent witnesses.

Hugo went outside ahead of her to get the tricycles out of the barn, thinking that he had not ridden his for some time. As it had a motor attached to it to help him when he needed it, and to propel him when he was feeling particularly feeble, it would probably take some starting. He'd eventually become used to using the conveyance and had found it a very useful means of transport.

He walked into the barn, and experienced one of those moments of paralysis which were becoming quite the thing at this address. He felt like his eyes were standing out on stalks. How could this be? How could such an event have occurred?

The first intimation that Lady Amanda had of the situation was a hurtling – within the limit of his physical capabilities – Hugo, gabbling incoherently, an anxious Tabitha in his wake.

'Slow down, Hugo,' advised Lady A, thinking that this was the first time she had ever had to use such a phrase with regard to her old friend. 'Whatever is the matter with you?'

'The tri ... the tri ... the tricycles have been st-st-stolen,' he puffed, doing his best to be coherent. 'They're g-g-gone from the b-b-b-a-rn.'

'Nooo!' She replied. 'Whoever would take those, when there are so many other more valuable objects to make away with?'

'Don't know!' wheezed Hugo, still struggling to get his breath.

At that moment, Lady A became aware of another huffing figure by her elbow, and swivelled slightly to find a winded Moody by her other side, obviously bursting with news. 'Well, what is it, man?' she queried, impatiently.

'I regret to inform you that the exterior entrance to the cellarage has been breached,' he informed her in a doleful voice but, strangely, he smiled as he spoke.

'So that means that anyone...' Her voice trailed

off in horror.

'It means that anyone could have gained access to your house and helped themselves to anything they fancied. I suggest you get that foppy houseman of yours to check out anything of particular value, just to make sure you've still got it.'

His gloomy summing up of the situation galvanised her into action, and she became a portly blur as she buzzed down the hall to find Beauchamp and send him on a treasure hunt to take register of her valued belongings.

A few minutes later the three of them, now minus the DI, had gathered glumly in the morning room and Lady A rang for morning coffee with the thought that Beauchamp could delay his mammoth search until he had supplied these three downcast souls with something sustaining. She only hoped the man would have sufficient common sense to provide a good solid selection of biscuits with which to accompany the beverage, as they all needed a bit of bucking up.

When the manservant finally arrived with his laden tray, his facial expression did not bode well. 'Good grief, Beauchamp! Whatever is the matter now? Has somebody died?... Apart from that unfortunate man upstairs, I mean.'

'No, your ladyship,' replied Beauchamp dolefully, without the slightest desire to cough 'Beecham' into his hand, and hoping that this would not still be true after he had imparted the news he bore so heavily in his heart. He really ought to revive 'Beecham Tennis'.

'However, I regret to inform you that the collection of Meissen figures that used to grace the library is no longer present, nor the Worcester collection from your late father's study.'

'What? Nooo. They *can't* be gone! They took *generations* to collect. They must have been *moved.* They *really* can't have been *taken.* Some of them were *unique* – the only example left in the world. Where are my smelling salts? Call for a doctor. I think I'm going to have a seizure.' It was the closest she had ever found herself to a swoon in her life.

Hugo rushed to her side on the central sofa and took her hand, immediately beginning to pat it to revive her. 'There, there, dear Manda. Don't take on so. You're adequately insured, so there should be no financial loss.'

'No financial loss? That means nothing. Those collections were irreplaceable. Some pieces were the only surviving examples known.'

'Why weren't they kept in the bank, then?' asked Tabitha, in all innocence.

'In the bank? In the bank?' spluttered Lady Amanda. 'And just how is one supposed to enjoy the beauty of a unique object when it's locked away in the darkness *in a bank,* you bloody foolish woman?'

Tabitha promptly did a perfect imitation of a beetroot, and retired from the room in some confusion.

'Manda! Manners!' Hugo upbraided her. He had no idea that she'd overheard his conversation with his sister about him residing at Belchester Towers, or how it had upset her.

'Well, did you ever hear such a plebeian idea in your entire life?'

'Sometimes she speaks without thinking.'

'Does she even know how to? – think, that is. And speaking of plebeians, get that blasted idiot of a policeman in here. He needs to know about this. Damn and blast it! With him in charge of the investigation, we'll never see hide nor hair of any of the pieces again. And, no doubt, he'll have the place swarming with that bloody soccer team again,' she concluded, with a rather mangled reference to the SOCO team that would, no doubt, be needed.

'And he'd better be quick about it, because I've got the Filth-Busters coming in tomorrow,' she added, referring to a large group of local ladies who came to the house at regular intervals to give it a good going over and stop the dirt from building up too much.

She managed to impress upon Moody the necessity for moving swiftly, and he had a team in the house within the hour, swarming all over it and generally getting in everyone's way, destroying any chance there was of privacy, and leaving grey powder over more than it appeared they needed to.

Having heard Lady Amanda's announcement of the invasion of the cleaners the next day, Tabitha asked her, 'Why don't you just have more live-in staff, then you wouldn't have so much upheaval, doing it only now and again?'

'Because,' replied Lady A, 'my mother discovered that they're more trouble than they're worth, as my father was always playing catch-me-if-you-can with the maids, and then not running very fast.' As she said this, she gave a furtive glance in the direction of Beauchamp, who flicked her a snide sneer. If her father hadn't had the irresistible urge to play hunt-the-sausage with the maids, he would not even exist.

His glare was also prohibiting, as he did not want her to go into more detail in front of Tabitha. After all, his actual origins had only come to light to Lady Amanda in quite recent times, but she knew when to zip her lip.

After all the turmoil of everything being dusted for fingerprints, and every last nook and cranny being turfed out, the whole household decided on an early night again, before the onslaught of cleaners on the morrow, and Belchester Towers was in darkness well before its usual hour, that day.

Thursday

The house was alive with alien bodies again, from quite early the next morning, but this time they wore headscarves and pinafores, rather than white protective overalls, and the sound of shrill female chatter filled the air as the women went about their tasks to the inevitable hum of vacuum cleaners.

Unexpectedly, a blood-curdling scream rent the air, and all activity within its range ceased, as minds cast about for a simple explanation of such a phenomenon. Perhaps one of the ladies had encountered a particularly muscular spider. Maybe a huge moth had flown out of some long-undisturbed curtains. Maybe one of the many ghosts said to haunt the place had put in an appearance.

Whatever had caused it, the cry had definitely come from the music room, but the hired help left it to the residents to investigate. None of them wanted to get caught up in anything unpleasant when they were only paid by the hour, and hired by the day.

When Lady Amanda entered the room, having overtaken Hugo in the corridor and espied Tabitha lurking in the recess under the stairs, she found Beauchamp already there, waiting for her with a grave expression on his face.

'What is it, Beauchamp? Whatever's happened?' Really, she was out of breath yet again. How hurried everything seemed since Hugo's sister's arrival under her roof.

'I'm afraid there has been a fatality in the ranks of the temporary staff, your ladyship,' he replied apologetically, as if the occurrence were his fault.

'No good! You'll have to try again; this time in English.' She never minced her words, and had no intention of starting now.

'One of the cleaners has been murdered, your ladyship,' explained the manservant, in easier to understand terms.

'Well, why didn't you just say so? Where? And how?'

'Behind the sofa, and with the A flat clarinet, in my opinion.'

'And, no doubt, by Colonel Mustard. Blast! That was a really good instrument,' expostulated Lady A, heading towards the named piece of furniture to take a quick peek. 'Yes. See what you mean. The thing's broken in two, with bloodstains on some of the keys.

'That's definitely beyond the skill of a repairer. And it was such a pleasure to play. On the other hand, thank the good Lord whoever it was didn't use the E flat. That's irreplaceable.' Not a word did she utter about the corpse that also lay there on display.

'Better get those police johnnies back again, with all those other chaps that have to go round after them to make sure they haven't made a mess.' She understood perfectly well the job of a SOCO team, but occasionally liked to play the ignoramus, just for fun.

Beauchamp bowed his head slightly in acknowledgement of her instruction, turned on his heel and left the room, just as Hugo and Tabitha were arriving. 'Hello, you last-minute-Larries. Got here just in time not to be involved in sorting out what should be done and what exactly happened, haven't you? Cowardy, cowardy custards! Can't cut the mustard!'

It must have been Tabitha's presence that had thrown Lady A straight back to the playground and the insults of childhood. 'Really, Manda!' Hugo admonished her, 'Tabitha is your guest, not a fellow schoolgirl. Where are your manners?'

'In the dim and distant past, I fear, Hugo. I'm just a little rattled.'

'Why? What's happened?'

'Not only has one of the cleaners gone and got herself murdered, but whoever did it clubbed her to death with my favourite A flat clarinet. They could at least have had the consideration to use the ratsy old C one. I hardly ever play that in church, and it's a bit of a cheap and nasty dog, anyway.'

'Manda! I'm ashamed of you. You seem to feel more for the instrument than you do for the victim,' replied Hugo, scandalised.

'Well of course I do. I really loved that clarinet. I didn't know the cleaner from Adam. Or Eve, I suppose I should say. She's just a woman from Belchester; but the clarinet has been in my possession for decades.'

As he was thus upbraiding her, Enid came bustling in, and headed straight for the sofa, peering behind it with trepidation. 'Oh, no!' she exclaimed.

'I know,' agreed Lady A. 'It was absolute heaven to play.'

'I meant the woman, Amanda. Really, sometimes I can't understand how your mind works,' replied Enid, horrified that her friend's first thoughts had been for the inanimate object rather than the person.

'Sorry. Do you know her?' asked Lady A.

'It's poor old Florrie Searle,' she replied. 'We went to school together. She was ever so good at impressions – used to have us all in fits of laughter, doing all the teachers and our parents.'

'Her last impression seems to have been of a corpse, but it's a jolly convincing one. I'm terribly sorry, everyone, but I think I'll go and have a bit of a lie down before the police arrive again. I seem to be suffering from a terrible case of bad taste,' admitted Lady A, who, for once, had actually listened to what she had just said.

At that, she abruptly about-turned and

marched out of the room, her head hung low and her shoulders hunched, apparently in shame, but Hugo could have sworn that her shoulders were shaking slightly, as if with laughter. She definitely needed a lie down, and some time to pull herself together. She looked slightly hysterical at all that had happened in the last twenty-four hours.

She must be in a severe state of shock, with the discovery of two corpses in the house, the access to the basement from the outside breached, and the loss of all the good plate, the Meissen and the Worcester collections, with goodness knows what else still to come; and to crown it all, the destruction of her A flat clarinet. That seemed to be the straw that had broken the camel's back.

Lady Amanda re-joined the others in the music room when she heard the police at the door, noticing, as she seated herself in an armchair, that the others had become less squeamish in her absence. There was not a lot of seating in this particular reception room, as it was mostly for practice and recital, and temporary seating could always be imported for the latter, when necessary, which was not often these days.

When the two detectives were ushered in by Beauchamp, there were only two spindly upright chairs left unoccupied. DS Glenister immediately perched his slim frame on the furthest, then eyed his senior officer with interest. Moody was by no means of slight build; in fact he carried quite a paunch on him, and the thought of him perched on the fragile little chair brought a sly grin to the sergeant's lips.

Moody eyed up his hostess, considering that if the frail-looking construction were unlikely to support his weight, she would not countenance sitting by while he did so. It must, therefore, be strong enough to bear him, and he lowered himself delicately on to its tapestry-covered seat.

A bright tinkling air immediately filled the room, and all eyes turned to Moody, as the music seemed to be issuing from his backside. Lady Amanda allowed herself a small smile as the inspector leapt from his dainty perch as if it were wired into the electricity supply.

A little unbelievingly, he tried to take a seat again and, once more, delicate music filled the air. He rose again, muttering, 'What the devil's going on?'

'Do take my seat, dear Inspector,' purred Lady A, rising and crossing the room. 'It would seem that you have, by chance, sat in the musical chair that belonged to a long-departed relative. I shall de-activate the mechanism and sit there myself. I feel that 'Bluebells of Scotland' is not a suitable accompaniment to what is to follow.'

Moody's face blushed like a huge, peeled blood orange, as he swapped seats with her, his dignity shattered, his authority non-existent, now. She'd done it again! Made him look a fool in front of potential witnesses! DS Glenister had to stuff his knuckles into his mouth to stop himself from laughing out loud.

'I don't know,' Moody blustered. 'I seem to visit this place more often than I visit the bathroom. You're a one-woman crime-wave, Lady Amanda' – the title nearly choked him – 'and that goes for your doddering old boyfriend as well.'

'I say!' spluttered Hugo. 'Steady on, there! I'm not her boyfriend: never have been and never will be.'

'Hugo!' exclaimed Lady A, sensing an insult where none was intended.

'Well, you know what I mean,' was all he said by way of explanation, but it seemed to do the trick.

'Point taken!' she observed, in a much calmer voice.

Lady Amanda may never have found men to her liking, but then, never had she felt any attraction to women either, and she and Hugo were identical in this respect. Although neither of them had ever considered the idea, they were probably both asexual, and perfectly happy with their lot in life.

After an awful lot of hot air, which the inspector would have called 'questioning', Lady A finally asked, 'But who on earth would want to kill a cleaner? And who was that chap in the suit of armour yesterday? None of this makes sense.'

Beauchamp returned to the music room at that moment and announced that one of the uniformed officers had been taking an e-fit of yesterday's corpse round the staff, both the outdoor and temporary indoor members, and there was now a name for the man in the metal suit.

'It would appear that he is, or was, a member of staff here, albeit a casual one, and his name was Victor Mangel. He used to work here full-time before he reached retirement age, then we kept him on for casual work as he was still desirous of continuing to work in the grounds.'

''Straordinary names domestics have these

days.' This was Hugo, nipping back to live in the past for a few moments. 'They used to be called things like Jones or Parker.'

'Stuff that, Hugo!' Lady Amanda had seen another side to this particular coin. 'What the hell was he doing on the inside of the house and, in particular, actually inside a suit of armour? There's something very fishy going on here. And now a maid's been murdered. And with my darling A flat clarinet!'

Her return to sadness was brought to an abrupt halt by a sudden yell of fury which reached their ears, albeit diluted by distance, and it acted as a summoning towards the kitchen, whence the cry of fury and despair had appeared to emanate.

On arrival, they found Enid standing with her head in her hands, and a pot of soup, with large spilled pools all around it, on the kitchen table.

'Whatever has happened, Enid?' asked Lady Amanda, eyeing up the mess, devoid of ideas for a suitable explanation.

'When I heard this weird noise behind me, I turned round and found it was those two feline monsters, their heads in the saucepan, licking away as if they hadn't been fed for weeks. One of them even had a front paw in the pan. The soup's ruined now – contaminated by their unhygienic tongues. God knows where those tongues had been last,' she added, a moue of distaste on her face at the very thought.

'I'm going to have to start all over again and make some more and, what's more, I've got no idea whatsoever where they've disappeared to. They could be making all kinds of havoc anywhere in the house, for all I know. They might even have got outside,' wailed Enid.

'My poor babies – outside in the big, bad world,' moaned Tabitha, in distress.

'Poor babies, my bum!' scoffed Lady A. 'They'll be somewhere inside smashing very expensive things, I'll be bound.'

'Shoot!' snorted Hugo, a hand up to his mouth.

'What is it, old thing?'

Hugo had turned a very fetching shade of crimson, and had to admit that, out of sheer vanity, he'd got his tartan trews out before he'd got dressed that morning, just to try them on again and have a look in his cheval glass, and he'd not put them away again.

Aware that he was going to be late for breakfast if he didn't get a wiggle on, he had merely draped them over the bed, to be attended to later, and the catch on his door was proving very temperamental at the moment. He said he'd put money on that being where the foul fiends were this very minute. The Law of Sod dictated it.

The posse formed and made a beeline for his room. Lady A – who had paid for the afore-mentioned article of clothing – in the front, her face as grim as that of an avenging sheriff on the trail of his man.

Hugo proved to be very good at guessing games, and the two tiny tartan terrorists were in the act of shredding the bottom of the right leg of said trews.

Simultaneously, Hugo screeched, 'Oh my God, no!' Lady Amanda carolled, 'I'll replace them, Hugo!' and Tabitha burst out with, 'My poor darlings! Come to Mother,' as she grabbed the two tiny bodies and held them protectively to her chest, turning to face the opposite direction to her hostess, whose face promised immediate execution, without benefit of trial.

As she rushed the guilty parties from the room, Hugo turned a devastated face to Lady A, who reassured him they'd be replaced in no time then added, just to let him see this particular cloud's silver lining, 'Just imagine the indescribable mess they'd have made if you'd had a kilt, and there'd been a sporran for them to shred. We'd have been up to our eyebrows in fur and stuff.'

'*Can* I have a kilt and a sporran this time, if I promise never to let her visit again?' he pleaded, real longing in his eyes.

'Of course you can, old chap. We'll get you measured up, and I'll get things underway as soon as possible.'

'Thank you so much, Manda. I've always wanted one.'

'You'll have the whole rig-out: after all, you only live once, so you should have as much of what you really want, while you can.'

'Oh, scrumptious, Manda!'

Chapter Five

While the two detectives liaised with the same SOCO team that had visited the day before, the members of which were becoming very familiar with the layout of Belchester Towers, uniformed officers had questioned the other staff who would only be here for the day.

They were very lucky to have been able to carry out this activity out of view of Lady Amanda, who would, no doubt, have given them a protracted lecture on wasting the time of members of staff who were paid by the hour, and who would not be present tomorrow. She would have declared most vehemently that she was not made of money, and didn't have funds to cover time spent chatting with officers of the law.

As it was, they were able to carry out this task in relative peace, and now reported back to Inspector Moody.

'Whom have you interviewed?' asked the inspector, showing a sensitivity to correct grammar with which Lady A would not have credited him.

'In the grounds, Evergreen the head groundsman, and Drake, Darke, and Darle.' This was followed by a facial expression of incomprehension, but no one questioned it, so the speaker didn't explain it.

'That must be fun when it comes to making up the pay-packets,' observed the senior officer.

'All paid into their bank accounts automatically,' Lady A informed him, pouring cold water on his weak witticism.

'Obviously. And what are the first names of these four individuals, PC Spouph?' What a silly name, he thought. It didn't ought to be allowed in the force, to have a silly name like that.

'For the last three, Ed, Edds, and Eddie. Evergreen wouldn't even admit to having a first name, sir.'

'What? Would you mind elaborating on the first three. They must be contractions, and as for Evergreen, how did he explain himself?'

'Edgar, Edmund, and Edward.'

'Making?'

'Edgar Drake, Edmund Darke, and Edward Darle, and Evergreen said to treat him like Inspector Morse orf the telly. He wasn't admitting to even having a first name, sir.'

'Put him down as Endeavour Evergreen, then. His wish is granted. How the hell have you let this situation occur?' he asked, spearing Lady Amanda with a beady eye.

'I don't care what they call themselves, as long as they do their job satisfactorily, and provide me with enough information to pay them and, as a matter of fact, his initial is E. I had to get that out of him to make regular payments into his bank account, so for all I know your facetious suggestion may even be correct,' she informed him, in a somewhat haughty manner.

How was it, he thought, that she always managed to make him feel small and inferior, socially? It happened every time he came into contact with her, and he had to go home and work on raising his level of self-confidence again before he could do anything else. Glenister seemed to be totally immune to it, and seemed to get on with her very well, damn and blast his trendy paisley socks.

'Well, come on then; what did you learn about the dead man?' snapped Moody, not caring who he took out his bad temper on.

PC Spouph took out his notebook and consulted it with all seriousness. 'He had been a permanent gardener here until a few years ago,' he intoned in a monotonous voice. 'When he retired, he was kept on the casual and emergency staff, able to be called in when there was a particular clear-up to do, or when a new project was planned, or even storm damage. And stuff like that,' he finished, rather lamely.

'Personal details, Constable! Was he married? Where did he live? Come on, come on!'

'He was widowed,' Spouph informed the inspector, the colour draining from his face at the ferocity of the senior officer's manner. That posh woman must have really got to him with whatever she said. 'He lived in a cottage in Plague Alley...'

'Enid must have known him, then. That's where she lives,' interrupted Lady A, not adding 'for now' so as not to arouse any curiosity in those not already in the know about her impending move to the big house.

'He's got no kids, but he is on police records for petty theft, although that was some years ago, now.'

'I know about that,' the woman interrupted him again. 'I took him on to give him another chance in life, as it's not easy to find work if you're an ex-con, as Inspector Moody will well know.'

'Very generous of you, I'm sure,' that individual snarled sarcastically.

'I never had any trouble with him the whole time he worked here. That's why I let him stay on as casual labour after retirement age, with Evergreen's blessing, of course. It is after all, his garden, and he must be allowed some say in who works in it with him, don't you think?'

She was proving all too magnanimous for Moody's liking, so he turned his attention, once more, to PC Spouph. 'Anything else?'

'H-h-he drank in The Witches' Cauldron, just off the Market Cross, and he played for their darts team,' Spouph continued nervously.

'Right den of thieves that place is. There are more villains per square metre in there than there are in Brixton Prison. Anything else?'

'Not really, sir; not what you'd call relevant, anyway.'

'Well I'd like to inform you all that I've recently had a call on my mobile from the station, and it seems that Jimmy "the Jemmy" Aldridge was released from prison about a month ago, and has now been spotted in this area three times, the first being about ten days ago. Spot the connection!'

'So you think this "Jimmy the Jemmy" character is responsible for the robberies here, sir?' asked Glenister, speaking for the first time since he'd entered the room.

'I know damned well he's at the root of it. I can feel it in my water.'

Lady A turned slightly green at the mental image this conjured up, and looked away to regain her former equilibrium. 'Does this mean that you'll all be on the lookout for this Jimmy-jemmy person, and do you think he's our murderer?' asked Hugo, only slightly confused about the name of the released prisoner.

'Yes,' confirmed Moody, then continued with his interrogation of PC Spouph. 'What about the indoor staff? Names?'

'Searle, Haire, Sylvester, and Moth,' he replied,

tentatively. 'Searle being the dead woman.'

'Not a Victor amongst them, is there?' asked Moody, smirking, then noticing that no one else had a smile on their face, although some of them were old enough to remember Victor Silvester the band leader.

'No, sir, they're all women: Florrie Searle – deceased – Edie Haire, Beryl Sylvester, and Madge Moth.'

'And did you learn anything useful from them?'

'Only that the French windows in the music room were noticed to be open for a while this morning, which is unusual, but the woman who noticed it thought that Lady Amanda might be sorting out some music for a recital while she had a guest staying, and that the room may have been found to smell musty, as it hasn't been used for some time, and needed a quick airing.'

'Thank you, Spouph. Go back to the station, type up your interview notes, and put a copy of them on my desk, please.'

'Yes, sir. Certainly, sir,' agreed the PC, evacuating the room immediately at some speed, to fetch his bicycle from the barn, and relieved to be leaving such high rank to pick on someone else and leave him in peace. There was no way he wanted to be the centre of attention.

Since her arrival the day before, Tabitha had contacted an old school friend whom she hadn't seen since moving away from the area many years ago, and who had agreed to come over and pick her up for an afternoon out, along with her husband and daughter.

'By the way, Phyllida Draycott-Bayliss, her husband Ethelred, and their daughter Poppy are coming to pick me up about three. Ethelred lives in a *real* castle. Although most of it's apparently a nineteenth century re-build, it's been done accurately, and the place is a real fairy-tale structure, just like in the movies.' This was a definite pop at Belchester Towers and its lack of actual age, it having been completely built in the 1800s.

'So, no different to this, then, really,' replied Lady Amanda, acidly.

'It's a complete replica of what was there before,' protested Tabitha, in defence of her friend's husband's ancestral home.

'A fiction of some architect's imagination, then. If it's a replica, the old place must have fallen down, so how do they know what it looked like with any degree of accuracy?' Ooh, she was getting herself into a right aristocratic tizzy – there was a hissy fit in the offing.

'From historical records, old plans, and woodcuts. There's a tapestry that shows it in its entirety; there were just loads of old records to show what it used to look like.'

'Sure there were. And this is a new build. When, exactly, in the nineteenth century was it thrown up, this so-called exact replica?'

'The 1870s, I think.' Tabitha supplied the information haughtily.

'Well, this went up in the early 1800s, so Belchester Towers is, *actually,* older than this replica that you're getting all defensive over.'

'Yar, boo, and sucks to you, you jealous old trout,' replied Tabitha, thumbing her nose at her hostess like an ill-mannered child.

Hugo eventually brokered a peace deal, and it was amicably agreed (sort of) that the Draycott-Baylisses would be asked in to take a cup of tea when they arrived to pick up Tabitha, so that Lady Amanda could, at least, show off a small portion of her home to 'the opposition', as she saw them.

Just before she was about to go upstairs to get changed into something she considered suitable for welcoming guests, she overheard another conversation between Hugo and his sister, this time in the library.

'You don't think she has you here because she actually likes you, do you?' Tabitha's voice rang out scathingly.

'Don't be such a bitch. You really have turned into a right old cat,' Hugo replied in defence, and Lady A rushed off upstairs, with no wish whatsoever to hear a word more of this acrimonious exchange. She was really very fond of Hugo, and she didn't want his sister poisoning his mind against her. She'd have to think of something.

Not much later, the Draycott-Bayliss family rang the doorbell, with impeccable manners, dead on time, just as the clock was chiming, and Beauchamp ushered them in with the utmost obsequiousness, in an attempt to create the best impression possible for his employer.

Lady Amanda herself emerged down the staircase, dressed and made-up to the nines, in her best effort at a Hollywood entrance. As usual, she was let down by something completely beyond her control. Enid emerged through the door from the domestic quarters, two shadows shot out after her, and the next thing anyone else knew, there were two spotty animals swinging from Phyllida Draycott-Bayliss's handbag.

Poppy, who had seen them come out, out of the corner of her eye, screamed. Phyllida, aware that her bag had suddenly almost doubled in weight, looked down, and sank to the floor in an excellent Victorian swoon, while Ethelred expostulated, 'Good Lord!' in the sort of accent that would have made Prince Charles sound as if he came from a sink estate.

Lady A rather ruined the effect she had created with her entrance by bellowing, 'Tabitha!' in the harsh and loud tones of a fishwife then, realising what she had done, rearranging her face into the semblance of a welcoming smile again, and continuing her elegant sway to the bottom of the stairs.

Finally, she extended a hand and approached the visitors to her home, as Tabitha shot out into the entrance hall, grabbed her little darlings – demons – gabbled a brief greeting to her old school-friend and family, and shot through the baize door to return her furry charges to their incarceration in the dog cage.

Enid was left muttering incoherent apologies about how the cunning animals had lifted the latch again on the cage, and escaped just as she was leaving, finally overtaking her as she reached the door from the domestic quarters to the hall. She was mortified at the situation that only looked to be her fault, as she knew who would get the blame when it came time for the kangaroo court, later.

Apart from her one screamed exclamation, Lady Amanda acted as if nothing had happened and, when Tabitha emerged through the baize door to the hall again, gave her a murderous look, daring her to say anything about the occurrence. Luckily, Tabitha knew how to read her of old, and sensibly decided to save her apologies for when her visitors were off Belchester Towers land.

Lady A conducted the three strangers to the drawing room to take tea, as if she were escorting royalty to a regal banquet. She had no sooner directed everyone to suitable seats, when Beauchamp entered, steering the tea trolley before him. 'Tea is served, your ladyship,' he announced in his most refined voice, and placed the comestibles' conveyance before his mistress.

At that moment, there was a noise that indicated that the baize door, heavy as it was, had been flung back as far as it would go, and a furious voice yelled, 'You come back here, you hairy little bastards!' It was no surprise whatsoever, then, when Ludovic and Dominic galloped into the room, leapt, and landed right on the tea trolley, in search of sanctuary.

Lady Amanda screamed as scalding hot tea streamed off the trolley and onto her skirt, Hugo yelped as the milk jug landed in his lap, and everyone present look astounded as the person from whom the yell had emanated entered the room in hot pursuit, and proved to be Enid Tweedie.

'Really, my dear!' Lady A chided her. 'Language!'

'Well, those two little buggers are enough to try the patience of a saint. If they aren't removed from where I spend most of my time soon, I swear I'll dice them and put them in a stew.'

'My poor precious ones!' moaned Tabitha, appalled at the thought of her darling charges being murdered, and left the room to try to incarcerate them again, hopefully with more success than the previous attempts had achieved.

On her return, she said, 'I used a bit of butcher's string to tie the catch into position this time. Unless they know how to undo knots, then we won't be disturbed again. I apologise unreservedly to you all, and I shall leave much sooner than planned, Manda.'

'Good!' was all her hostess managed, preparing to leave the room in search of a clean skirt, and some Germolene for her poor, burned knees.

Hugo made the offer of a fresh pot which, he assured the guests, would be ready in two shakes of a lamb's tail, but they very politely – and rather coldly – declined, saying that they must get off, or there wouldn't be time to show Tabitha the whole of their dear old castle.

Suddenly, Enid and Hugo found themselves totally alone in the vastness of the drawing room. 'Bum!' said Hugo, with feeling.

'Double bum!' replied Enid, in complete agreement with his sentiments.

For the rest of the day, the house and grounds swarmed with policemen.

Chapter Six

Friday

The next morning, there was no need for alarm clocks, as a shrill scream from outside woke everybody with unappreciated abruptness. It then continued, like a human siren, and three figures appeared on the landing in their night-clothes, worried expressions on their faces.

Tabitha sported a floor-length, long-sleeved flannelette garment with a ribbon for decoration just below her chin; Lady Amanda wore sensible flannelette pyjamas, both mindful of how cold the nights still were, and the fact that the heating was not run throughout the night. Hugo was the most surprisingly attired, in a mid-calf-length blood-red nightshirt, matching night-cap and bedsocks, and both ladies stared at him in utter astonishment. If the thought had ever crossed their minds at all, they would have judged him to be a predictable striped pyjama man.

'What are you two staring at?' he asked, as they all headed for the staircase, to descend and identify the source of the noise.

'You!' declared his sister. 'What do you look like?'

'I thought you were Jean-Paul Gaultier!' said Lady A sarcastically, with a snicker.

'Yes, indeed!' said Tabitha. *'Très chic, mon frère!'*

'Oh, shut up and concentrate on where you're going, or you'll end up in plaster of Paris, but with no opportunity to practise the language.'

Lady A reached the foot of the stairs first, put her head down, and raced, as if she was trying to score a try at rugby, towards the front door. She stopped at this point and looked outside, to see two figures standing at the foot of the steps. The other two pulled up behind her as she identified the pair as Beauchamp and Enid Tweedie, and Enid had a lit cigarette in her hand. What the...?

'What the hell do you think you're doing, Enid? You don't smoke!'

'I used to years ago, and I've felt the need to start again – only temporarily, you understand – since Hugo's sister arrived with her two hell-cats; and now I've found a dead body in the shrubbery.'

'Where?' asked three voices in unison. Surely there couldn't be a third corpse on the premises in three days?

'Just opposite the doorway, where the drive bears left, in the evergreen bushes. I'd just come outside for a pre-breakfast puff, and I saw her foot protruding from the greenery and, when I went over to investigate, thinking someone was hiding there, there she was, dead as a doornail.'

'Pre-breakfast?' queried Hugo. It was still dark, but then it was always dark when he got up, at this time of the year.

'It is half past five,' Beauchamp informed him, in a dignified manner.

'Half past what?' questioned Lady Amanda. 'I didn't know there were two half past fives in a day,' she said, scandalised at the earliness of the hour.

'Look on the bright side, Manda,' Hugo counselled her.

'What bright side?' she asked, amazed that he could detect the existence of such a thing.

'They'll have to get that Moody out of bed to "attend the scene",' he explained, lapsing into police jargon, and causing an absolute flurry of inverted commas.

'So they will!' she crowed, and a cruel smile crossed her face; 'and we can all go back to bed – apart from Beauchamp and Enid. Sorry, you two.'

Enid puffed greedily at her cigarette, and asked, 'Didn't you know what time Beauchamp got up to get the house ready? I've been coming up here at the same time, before I've even had a cup of tea, to give him a hand. You really do need some more indoor staff. Neither of us is as young as we used to be.'

'I had no idea!' exclaimed Lady A, with a horrified face. 'I'll get on to the Agency as soon as these murders are cleared up. But it'll have to be daily staff. I don't want anyone else living in, apart from you two.'

'That will be perfectly acceptable, your ladyship. Thank you so much.'

'Who is this dead cove in the bushes?' At least Hugo was eager to find out who else had been murdered, even if no one else was.

'I didn't even take a proper look,' Enid admitted. 'I merely noticed that the body was female, then I got rather hysterical. I'm so sorry to have woken you. If only I'd kept calmer, we could have sorted this out without the need to rouse you three.'

'Don't worry, Enid. Moody's enough of a sadist

to make sure that waking us up was the first thing that he initiated when he arrived here. If he'd had to get up early, so would we. And with that thought in mind, I don't think it's worth us going back to bed. He'll only insist we get up again. Do you think you could make us a pot of tea, Beauchamp, there's a good chap? Then we can sort out our ablutions and dressing and come down for breakfast.'

Moody lived up to his name when he arrived, proving to be in a filthy mood after his unexpected early reveille. Glenister was one big yawn, but Moody was in mean mode, and waspish in his snarled remarks. 'And who exactly has been wiped out on your dangerous premises, now?' he asked sarcastically.

Beauchamp answered with as much dignity as he could muster. 'Her name is Edie Haire, and she was part of the casual cleaning team that was working here yesterday. I've checked for a pulse and found the body to be stone cold, so may I respectfully suggest that she was killed yesterday evening? If we take a look around, we should find her bicycle. She lived in Snuff Street, and always cycled when she worked here.' The manservant was perfectly calm, which was more than could be said for anyone else.

'Thank you very much, Sherlock bleedin' Holmes,' snapped Moody. 'There's no need to try to teach your grandmother to suck eggs, you jumped-up domestic lackey.'

Behind his back, Beauchamp behaved in a way Lady A had never witnessed before; he poked out his tongue and flipped the inspector the bird.

'Really, Beauchamp, what on earth do you think you're doing. This is most unlike you,' she opined in a harsh whisper.

'And you haven't exactly been your good-mannered self recently. Myself, I think we've all been affected by Miss Tabitha's visit. Even my Enid's resorted to the evil weed again,' he hissed back.

'Surely that's not cannabis she's smoking?' asked Lady Amanda in alarm.

'Of course not! The evil weed I was referring to was tobacco. She gave up thirty years ago. I just hope she can kick the habit again when Mr Hugo's sister leaves, which I hope is very soon. Her new pets are not easy to live with.'

'Do you know, I think you're right, Beauchamp. I have been aware of not being impeccably mannered, the last few days, and I honestly believe you've hit the nail on the head.'

'Oi, Lady Muck!' Moody was doing his Prince Charmless act again.

'Yes, Inspector, dear,' replied Lady A, determined to behave herself after her enlightening conversation with Beauchamp.

'I want name, address, and anything you know about the stiff, and I'll get the SOCO back yet again. They'll be arriving here every morning automatically, if you have any more corpses for us.'

Still behind him, the manservant put a thumb to the end of his nose and wiggled his fingers. He then proceeded to bite his thumb at the man – the oldest insulting gesture he knew – let the man have a bit of Shakespearean abuse.

'Inside, you two,' barked Lady A, pointing towards the front door with a thumb, and found she was left alone with DS Glenister, as DI Moody went off with his mobile phone to play Mr Self-Important as he summoned the SOCO team, once again, to his side.

'Got any post-mortem results or forensics for me?' she asked a yawning Glenister in a low voice, leaning furtively closer to him.

'I have, as a matter of fact,' he replied, keeping his tone low, too.

'Dish the goss, then, young man,' ordered his companion, her face alight with enthusiasm.

The first meal of the day was taken, as usual, in the little room known as the breakfast room, and Lady Amanda was bursting with news, which she had had to suppress until they were all together and in private. Unusually, for this meal of the day, Beauchamp and Enid had been invited to join the other three, so that they could all commune as a group.

'Right, you lot,' Lady A called them all to order as Beauchamp poured the tea and Enid poured coffee for those who preferred it. 'That nice Glenister chappie has spilled the beans, so when I've passed on what he told me we should be as up to date as that Moody twit.'

'You're surely not thinking of getting involved in murder yet again?' asked Hugo, aghast. They'd already found themselves caught up in three incidences of unlawful killing, entirely due to her insatiable curiosity and sheer nosiness.

'But, of course, Hugo. These murders have been carried out actually on my premises. How could I resist the temptation, with everything going on right under my nose?'

'What's all this about getting involved with murder cases? It sounds most unsuitable and thoroughly unladylike,' enquired Tabitha, who was not privy to any details of their previous detecting activities.

'Just a little hobby of ours: solving murder cases for the police.' Lady A used this as a throw-away line, in her efforts to sound cool, and increase her house points for her street-cred tally. All she actually achieved was to induce a case of mild hysterics in her guest, who was absolutely horrified at the thought of her big brother – her now elderly brother – putting himself in dangerous situations, and getting involved with killers.

'Don't fuss so, Tabby. We haven't been in that much danger,' he tried to calm her, but remembering some of the tight corners they'd got themselves into, especially in their last case in Rumdrummond Castle over Burns Night, he knew this to be a lie, and he crossed his fingers childishly, in retrospect.

'That confirms it! So, you have been put in danger by this reckless old bag.'

'Tabby!' Hugo admonished her in a loud voice.

'You always were a cow at school, and time hasn't mellowed you one jot,' Lady A shot back, undoing all the good work that not seeing each other since they had been at school together had wrought.

'That does it! I'm leaving straight after this meal, and I want you to come with me, Hugs!' she declared, in a haughty manner.

'Not on your life, Tabs. I'm staying put. We never got on like a house on fire, and I'm having a lot of fun living here and getting mixed up in all sorts,' retorted Hugo, suddenly realising that he had been having the time of his life, despite his half-hearted protests.

'You do as you please. You always were an ungrateful old sod.' With that, Tabitha shoved a whole half-slice of toast in her mouth, rose, and marched out of the room, mumbling round her edible oral obstruction, 'And I shan't be coming back in a hurry. I shall be glad to get away from this mad-house where nobody's safe, and somebody loses their life every day.'

'I bet you're covered in crumbs after that little speech,' Lady A called after her, utterly determined to have the last word, although she was almost certain that the words 'Up yours!' floated ethereally on the wind in the distance. But that didn't matter at all. Hugo had finally seen his sister in her true colours, and he was going to stay on here at Belchester Towers and join in with her latest investigation, which was just about to get underway.

Utterly unmoved by his sister's hasty departure, Hugo piped up, 'Come on, Manda, dish the dirt.'

With an equal lack of concern for their recently departed guest, Lady A's face broke into a huge smile of utter smugness, as she began, 'That lovely DS Glenister brought me completely up to date.

'It seems that the first victim, Victor Mangel, was shot and Florrie Searle suffered a heavy blow from a blunt instrument. Victor had been dead about a week, so he was definitely put in that suit of armour while we were in Scotland at dear Siobhan's.

'If that awful sister of yours hadn't brought those two wild cats into my house we would have eventually noticed the smell on the landing. The fact that the cats managed to topple over the suit of armour merely meant that he was found earlier.

Florrie Searle was simply bopped over the head, but that definitely happened yesterday morning, and it would seem that the killer probably came from outside – one of the staff noticed that the music room's French windows were open for a while during the pre-luncheon period, and we know none of us either opened or closed them.'

Three heads nodded in unison in agreement.

'What about that Jemmy fellow that Moody was going on about. Did the young sergeant have anything to say about him?' Hugo was showing a lively interest; this was more like it, rather than watching every word he said with his sister around.

'He said there have been two more sightings: one in The Witches' Cauldron, and one in the environs of the cathedral. Apparently Moody went to warn the bishop about this character, and the bish has fair got the wind up. He's locked up all the silver and valuables, so the cathedral's without its bling at the moment.'

It was another French word used in anger that put Lady Amanda into her next tizzy. About mid-morning, she was heading for the music room to collect her E flat clarinet, to have a bit of a blow and get her lip in again – for she was sure to have lost her embouchure since she had last played –

when *'merde'* was yelled in a furious voice that sounded to be Beauchamp's and to have come from the billiard room.

She rapidly changed direction and headed for the source of the Gallic anger, thinking that Beauchamp really seemed to be getting in touch with his roots now – as long as he kept doing hers with hair colour, she didn't mind what he got in touch with. It certainly wouldn't be his feminine side, now he was contemplating matrimony.

On entering the large room, she found her manservant leaning against the billiard table with his hands raked through his hair, a look of despair on his face. 'Whatever's the matter, man? You look like you've seen a ghost,' she asked.

He merely removed his right hand from his head and pointed at the glass-fronted cabinet where all the family's trophies and sporting cups had once been stored. 'They're gone! All gone!' he declared, his voice now no more than a croak.

Lady A's head swivelled in the appropriate direction with all the stilted movement of an automaton, demonstrating her reluctance to come across more malfeasance. The cupboard was, indeed, absolutely empty. Every trophy and cup that had been won by a family member since the house was built was now no longer on the premises. Someone had definitely had it on their toes with the evidence of the family's sporting prowess, and she was suddenly overcome with a wave of fury.

'Get that miserable specimen of a policeman in here!' she barked, her eyes flashing and her fists clenching and unclenching. 'Oh, and by the way, Hugo's sister is, I think, this very minute, packing to leave.' Beauchamp shook his head, as if emerging from a nightmare, and said, 'Does that mean Plumstead will be leaving, too?'

'Absolutely!'

'Thank God for that! The man's a right pain in the arse,' was the unexpectedly coarse reply, and Beauchamp scuttled from the room in search of the inspector, his face now split by a grim grin of satisfaction.

When that miserable specimen did present himself in the room, he had a nasty smile on his face that indicated some sort of triumph. Before Lady A could open her mouth, he was in there with his own snippet of news.

'I have good news and bad news for you. The good news is that your tricycles have been found.' Before she had the time to reply, he had added, 'Unfortunately they were at the bottom of the canal, and I'm afraid they're disgustingly dirty, and rather the worse for wear.'

'Then I certainly don't want them back here,' his opponent informed him in her most uppity voice. 'When you've finished with them, have them sent to a garage to be repaired and cleaned, and make sure they take extra care when cleaning the saddles. One never knows whose bottoms might have been on them in their absence. And now I should like to inform you that there has been yet another robbery.

'All the family's silver trophies from our sporting past have been stolen. This cabinet was full of them up to yesterday, and now every last one of them is gone. What are you going to do about this serial offending, eh? And these murders? They're turning into a daily occurrence now. What, exactly, are you doing about it?' she asked, showing that the boot was now on the other foot, and she'd turned the tables on him very neatly.

Before he'd had more than a minute or two to bluster, Glenister almost skidded into the room, so fast was he moving, his eyes full of news.

'He's been sighted again, guv, and actually coming out of the drive to this house,' he said, triumph in his voice. 'That's the third sighting in a few days, so Jimmy "the Jemmy" Aldridge is definitely *in* our manor, and has *been in* our manor – house. Geddit? Ha ha!'

His humour was not appreciated by his superior officer, who merely asked, 'When?'

'Last night, sir,' replied the younger man, now in more sober mode.

'Then that must have been when he murdered Edie Haire and stole all the trophies from this room.'

'I thought you had men on duty keeping watch, Inspector.'

'I did,' the man replied furiously, 'and I'll have their guts for garters.'

'Whatever's the world coming to, when we can't even rely on our policemen to be on the alert,' asked Lady A, mischievously.

'Oh, shut up, you old bag!'

'Sir, you said that out loud,' Glenister advised him.

'Oh, my Gawd!' Moody fled the room with a hand over his mouth, his face a picture of extreme embarrassment. He'd had no idea he'd actually articulated the thought.

Chapter Seven

'Evergreen, in the potting shed, with a cast-iron trug,' stated Lady Amanda, inexplicably.

'Pardon?' queried Hugo, totally confused.

'I'm very bored with this live action version of Cluedo and I need some new long janes. Mine are in such a state, they won't see me through the rest of the cold weather this year.'

'Brainwave, Manda. I could do with some more vests and winter drawers, myself. The bottom halves have worn very thin in places, and the top halves seem to have had a visit from a plague of moths.'

'I'll get Beauchamp to attend to your clothes storage areas to deal with the munching insects, and, this afternoon, we'll take a trip into Belchester and make a visit to Curt and Pawtly. They always come up with the right quality goods.'

'Can we have afternoon tea in The Copper Kettle? They do the most delicious crumpets and they've got Darjeeling.'

'Of course we can, silly Hugo. We'll have an extra-scrumptious tea to celebrate the departure of your ghastly sister.'

'I'm so sorry about her. She was a bit of a nightmare, wasn't she? And those awful cats! My poor trews! And she was a bit of a cow to me, too.'

'I must admit to overhearing a couple of conversations between the two of you and I wanted to go into the room and bloody her nose for her, but I didn't, because I didn't want to embarrass you.'

'And she kept calling me "Hugs". She hasn't done that since she was in the nursery. Yuk!'

'How galling. But I liked the way you referred to her as "Tabby" a few times; that's a cat's name, if ever I heard one, and she's a prize-winning cat, if ever I saw one. She ought to be registered with the Governing Council of the Cat Fancy: I can't say her pedigree's outstanding, but they'd probably accept it, at a push.'

As the tricycles had not yet been returned from their adventure in the canal, and subsequent incarceration at the police station as evidence, they got Beauchamp to drive them into the city centre in the Rolls.

He dropped them at the Market Cross, and they walked the short distance up West Street to their store of choice, Hugo sporting a pair of canes. 'What's with the sticks, old chap? I thought you were much better with getting around,' asked his fellow shopper.

'I was, but have you noticed that it's not just cold at the moment; we're having quite a bit of damp, too, and that really gets to my old bones. Remember, I've got another replacement next month, and we're nearly finished, but I still get achy bits, and a lot of them won't be being replaced with titanium ones – thanks for arranging the upgrade, by the way.'

'No problem. Titanium lasts much longer and is less likely to break, so it could save a lot of bother in the long run. Actually, I think I might sort out Grandmama's cane – the one with the silver dog's head, when we get back – I'm suffering a bit, myself, and could do with just a little extra support.'

'And I'm going to sort out the old Zimmer with the wheels and brakes, and do my old impression of Stirling Moss.'

'Didn't I get you a bicycle bell for that, so that you could warn people if you were charging up behind them?'

'You did, and your mother gave me an old-fashioned rubber bulb horn for it, too, so there shouldn't be any mishaps in the future.'

By now they were entering the large clothing store that was Curt and Pawtly, and Mr Curt himself – who had a cunningly placed mirror that showed him who had entered when he was at his desk in the back room – came out to greet two of his most important customers.

Rubbing his hands together, probably because the heating was having a job coping when the door had been opened, but giving a good impression of Uriah Heep being 'ever so 'umble', he came forward to shake their hands and enquire of what assistance he could be to them on this bitingly cold day.

'Vests and winter drawers, Mr Curt. Ours can't quite see us through to the end of this winter, so we've come to stock up early for the rest of this one and the next and save ourselves a trip in November.'

'Very sensible of both of you, Lady Amanda. If you would care to accompany me to the first floor in the lift, I'll show you what we have in stock, although we don't have quite our full range, this being the end of the season, so to speak.'

Heavy winter underwear had a small room of its own upstairs at this time of year, and included things like liberty bodices and winter-weight petticoats, bedsocks, nightshirts, pyjamas, and nightcaps, thus alerting Lady A to the fact that Hugo probably wasn't a stranger to these premises, and this was immediately confirmed by Mr Pawtly, who was behind the counter in the appropriate room.

'Why, good day to you, Mr Hugo, and may I say what a pleasure it is to see you again. You haven't been in for quite some time, if my memory serves me correctly.'

'You're quite right. I've not suffered from the best of health in recent years, but due to the ministrations of my very good friend here, I'm getting more mobile by the month, and getting back a very good quality of life.'

'Hello, your ladyship,' carolled Mr Pawtly, leaning over to one side to get a clearer view. 'I didn't see you there, screened as you were by Mr Hugo. How lovely to see you again. How may I help you?'

'Winter-weight vests and long drawers,' explained Hugo, this time, and Mr Pawtly began to pull out drawers from a whole wall of wooden-fronted compartments behind the counter.

'Now, if I remember rightly, your ladyship, you take a forty-four portly in vests, and an extra-large in long janes. Is that correct?'

'Spot on, sir. If I can take just one of each to try on and take with me today, I'll leave my order with you to be delivered, when you can get it together.'

'Excellent, your ladyship. Here are the garments

you require,' the man said, handing over the two items of underwear to Lady A, who scooted straight into a changing room, calling out to Hugo to hang on a minute before he tried on anything, as she had some special advice for him regarding these garments and the arrangements at Belchester Towers.

There was a good deal of huffing and puffing, as Lady A shed her outer clothes, and the odd muffled oath, as she got stuck in her petticoat, and blundered around the changing room for a few seconds, blind as a bat and thoroughly imprisoned.

After a particularly heart-felt 'Damn and blast', which no one but her knew involved having put on the new long janes back to front and, thus, having to start all over again, she emerged, a sight for sore eyes.

'Manda! You must have been given the wrong sizes,' expostulated Hugo, as his eyes nearly popped out of his head. Lady A had vest sleeves which completely covered her hands, and hung nearly to her knees. The legs of the long janes covered her feet with material to spare, and pulled right up to her armpits.

'I don't know what sizes you usually buy, Hugo, but this is the way you buy them if you want them to survive the Belchester Towers laundry service. It's fine for pre-worn clothes, but cruel to brand new ones. They fit perfectly after the first wash, but Beauchamp always washes bed linen, towels, and underwear on sixty degrees, which means that there is, inevitably, a certain amount of shrinkage. I've found that this is about right for me. Perhaps Mr Pawtly could do a calculation as to which sizes you should now require.'

'Already done, Mr Hugo. If you'd like to take these into a cubicle, I can assess whether I have worked the sizes out to allow adequately for shrinkage. Into a cubicle with you.' Mr Pawtly was getting quite playful, with a visit from two of his old customers whose requirements he understood perfectly.

After a couple of minutes punctuated only by moans and groans, as Hugo's joints made their disapproval felt about this second exercise in dressing, so soon after the first, Mr Pawtly called in, enquiring if he was ready to come out and show them how he looked.

'No!' came the reply.

'Why not?' queried the co-owner of the establishment.

'Come over here, so I can tell you,' requested Hugo in an embarrassed voice. Mr Pawtly approached the heavy curtain and put his ear to it,

'I can't come out there in my underwear. There's a girl out there. I've never appeared before a girl in my underwear before in my life, and I don't intend to start now. It's most unseemly.'

'Oh. Hugo, you are a shrinking violet. I'm going downstairs now, so give me a minute, and it'll be all clear for you to come out,' declared Lady A, putting a fist into her mouth to stop the laughter, as she made for the lift, to remove herself from Hugo's field of coyness.

Hugo's sense of outrage at the previously proposed invasion of his privacy while in unsuitable clothing had abated by the time they got to The Copper Kettle, and he was feeling much more his usual self when they were seated, waiting for their 'premium' afternoon tea.

Hugo changed his mind at the last minute, and it was a pot of Assam tea that was first delivered to their table, along with a covered metal dish full of hot, crispy buttered crumpets and soft brown muffins oozing with their generous helping of butter.

Lady Amanda took the role of 'mother' and poured for them both, while Hugo took on the role of 'chief glutton' and fairly dived into the metal dish to fill his plate, from which he immediately began to fill his face, allowing a liquid yellow trail to snake from his mouth down his chin.

'Manners!' his companion chided him, and he reached immediately for a napkin to wipe away the signs of his hasty consumption. 'Sorry, Manda, couldn't help myself. It must be all that changing in and out of underwear. I feel absolutely starving.'

'No change there, then, in the presence of comestibles. Hugo, let's take this opportunity of being away from home and all prying ears to have a quick sum up of what we know of the case so far, and what we should do next.'

'Oh, goody goody gumdrops! A special tea *and* plotting and planning on a new investigation. I must have died and gone to heaven!'

'You'll certainly die if you don't start focusing your mind – whether you'll go to heaven or not, I wouldn't care to offer an opinion.'

'OK. You do a précis of what we know so far, then we can work out what to do next.' This was a cunning move on Hugo's part, to be allowed to carry on eating, while his companion did all the yacking. That should see him through to when the cakes arrived, and he wasn't quite so hungry.

'Agreed.' How she did like the sound of her own voice. 'We've had three bodies. I've been thinking about that – the timing, and who they were, and I've concluded that they were killed for different reasons.'

'How do you work that out?' Hugo asked, his mouth full, with the inevitable result that he sprayed his front with crumbs and earned himself a dirty look for his lack of manners again.

'The first one in the suit of armour – Victor Mangel – I actually think he may have been involved in the original robberies, and it was a case of thieves falling out. He was killed so much earlier than the others, and in a different way. Maybe he'd been led astray again, after all these years. He can't have had much of a life since he retired, being widowed, and having no regular daily activity any more.'

'That's true. Maybe he was even responsible for whoever has been taking things and knocking people off with such abandon actually gaining access in the first place. Maybe he took on the role of a mole.'

'Well worked out, Hugo. I think you could be on to something there. Maybe he managed to unlock the basement access to the outside world before we went away, so that no breaking and entering was necessary – the entering was already arranged for whoever it was; presumably this Jimmy the Jemmy character.'

'And what about the two casual cleaners, then?

What made him kill them?'

'I'm not sure about Florrie Searle, that could be as simple as her overhearing a conversation and having to be silenced, but I think Edie Haire might have been leaving after working late, and caught sight of our thieving chap trying to gain entrance to the property.

'Maybe she even challenged him as to what he was up to, and he just brained her one and threw her in the shrubbery. The police eventually found her bicycle in the stables. If you remember, that was the night that all the sporting trophies were made off with, so he was probably trying to get in to conceal himself, until a convenient time to make away with them arose.'

'I say, you are good, Manda. I wouldn't have been able to imagine half that stuff,' Hugo said admiringly, as a huge plate of cakes was put down on the table, and the empty metal muffin dish removed. Hugo's eyes danced with greed as they surveyed the choice set before him.

'What I suggest we do, to try to winkle out some information, is speak to the other maids who were on duty that day. We can probably get their names and addresses from Beauchamp when he comes to pick us up. Then, tomorrow, we can have a casual chat with the outdoor staff; they were to be on duty for much longer, as the garden always needs a huge cut back and tidy up at this time of the year.

'Then I think we should embark on a spree of going out in the evenings to visit the local pubs and any eating places there are. This Jimmy the Jemmy isn't a local so, presumably, even if he's found digs, he'll go out in the evening, when he's not on a "job", for food and company.'

'But, we don't know what he looks like, Manda, and Moody's not going to want to help us out, is he?'

'No, but I bet that nice Sergeant Glenister would show us a photograph of him from police records, to give us some idea of who we're looking for, and he could do it on the quiet, so that none of us gets into trouble with old Grumble Guts.'

'Genius!' exclaimed Hugo, through a mouthful of fondant fancy.

'Really, Hugo, you've got crumbs all over *my* woolly. Please don't talk with your mouth full.'

'Sorry, Manda,' replied Hugo so promptly, that he sprayed her again, much to her disgust.

Beauchamp pulled up outside in the Rolls just at the point that Hugo thought that, if he ate another bite, he would burst. Lady A had been fidgeting for at least the last ten minutes, not having a stomach with the same large capacity as Hugo's, and not being a greedy-guts to boot, and could have cheered when she saw the familiar vehicle draw to a halt.

When they were comfortably installed in the rear seat, blankets solicitously thrown over their elderly knees, Beauchamp admitted that he could remember the names of the other maids and, as he had his iPad with him, he could access their addresses as well.

'Excellent fellow, Beauchamp. At least one of us in the household can claim to have joined the twenty-first century,' crowed Lady A.

'What's an iPad?' asked Hugo, a frown wrinkling his forehead even more severely than usual.

Beryl Sylvester, it turned out, lived in Scraggs Lane, which bordered the public gardens. Her house was found to be a pretty little cottage on the outside, which could do with considerable modernisation on the inside – great for photographically inclined visitors, but pretty miserable to live in.

'Oh, your ladyship!' she exclaimed with surprise, on opening her front door. 'Whatever are you doing on my doorstep, and Mr Hugo too?' – Beauchamp had remained with the car, not only for the sake of security, but because he knew how small those dwellings were on the inside.

'Do come in and let me get you some tea or something,' blustered Beryl Sylvester, thoroughly discombobulated by this unexpected visit of the aristocracy to her very humble abode.

'No thanks. We're fine,' Lady A refused politely, then continued, 'we'd just like to ask you a few questions about Florrie Searle and Edie Haire, if we may.'

'I'm afraid I don't know anything about their deaths,' Beryl replied then, remembering her manners, invited them to take a seat. 'You'll have to take me as you find me,' she said. 'This place is no palace, and the landlord hasn't done any modernisation since before the war. I've still got an outside toilet and a tin bath.'

'Give me his name and telephone number and I'll see what I can do,' replied Lady A, absently. 'No, I mean about their characters, and what you saw of them the day they died.'

'Thank you very much your ladyship,' said

Beryl, in reply to Lady A's offer of intervention on her behalf on the state of the house. 'This is the most neglected house in the lane, because all the others are privately owned, and not rented, like this one.

'As for Florrie and Edie, they did have one thing in common, although they displayed the trait in completely different ways,' explained Beryl.

'Go on,' Lady A encouraged her, thinking that they might be about to get somewhere.

'They were both terribly nosy. Florrie was probably the worst, though. If Edie wanted to know about something that was going on, she just approached the person who would know, and asked them outright.

'Florrie was more sneaky, and usually learnt things she wasn't supposed to hear by listening at doors, and eavesdropping whenever she had the opportunity. She also went through people's private papers and possessions if she got the chance. She was a menace, I thought – always spying.'

'Thank you very much, Beryl, my dear. You've been very helpful,' Lady Amanda praised her occasional cleaner, thinking that what they had just been told rather confirmed her theory that Florrie could have overheard something and been knocked on the head because someone had found out what she had done.

'Should you require regular hours at the Towers, please give Beauchamp a ring and ask him when he could find employment for you,' she concluded, remembering that she had promised she would recruit more staff to help out the soon-to-be-married couple.

Beryl's face lit up with delight at the thought of a regular income, and she pumped Lady Amanda's hand in genuine gratitude, when she and Hugo took their leave of her.

Their next port of call was a house in Beggars Run, near the Cat and Footstool public house and, there, in the picturesque black and white cottage, in far better repair than their last destination, they found Madge Moth, surrounded by library books on local history.

'We apologise for disturbing you without warning,' began Lady A, who found this member of staff stronger of character than Beryl Sylvester and even a little intimidating.

'No problem, your ladyship. I'm just doin' a bit o' readin' on the city's history,' replied Madge, indicating her collection of books.

'I can see that, and jolly academic it looks, too. The thing is, we're here to ask you about Florrie Searle and Edie Haire. Did you know them at all?'

'I was quite friendly with Edie Haire,' replied Madge, her expression turning doleful. 'We weren't what you'd call bosom buddies, but we got on all right. Florrie, I didn't get on with quite so well. She seemed to find me a little much, and used to scuttle off whenever I hove into view.'

'What can you tell us about their characters?' asked Hugo, suddenly realising that he hadn't uttered a word in the last house they had visited.

'They were both a bit of a gossip, if you know what I mean, but whereas Edie was upfront about it, and talked openly about anyone and anything she chose, Florrie was more underhand, whispering in corners about people and stuff, never coming out into the open about anything she knew.'

'That's very interesting, and fits in with what else we know of the two women's characters,' said Lady Amanda. 'Thank you very much for your time.'

'Are you sure you won't stay for a cup of tea and a slice of my home-made fruit cake?' asked Madge hospitably.

'So kind of you, but we've just taken afternoon tea,' Lady A refused politely, while Hugo turned green at the very thought of consuming more, and rushed on ahead outside for some fresh air before he was sick from overeating.

Chapter Eight

They had chattered like hyper-active schoolchildren on the way home in the back of the car, believing that they had sorted out motives for all the murders so far. But they would have to clear their minds of such mundane matters this evening, for it had been designated a wedding planning night, where Beauchamp and Enid would put forward their wishes for the big day, and Lady A would add her two-penn'orth or, perhaps, rather more, they hoped.

After dinner, they took their coffee in the drawing room so that they didn't waste any more time at table, and Beauchamp started off, explaining what they had already done.

'We've booked St Michael-in-the-Fields for the

first Saturday in April, at two o'clock. We've been to see the vicar, and booked the bells and the choir. Enid hasn't found an outfit yet, but there's plenty of time for that, and it's only the celebrations afterwards to arrange now, apart from some minor details,' he informed his listeners.

'I'd forgotten that you could get married in church because Enid's a widow and you, of course, have never been married before, Beauchamp,' said Lady Amanda. 'And as for the nuptials feast,' she continued, making Enid blush at the very thought of nuptials, 'I should like you to have that here, as my wedding present to you both.'

Enid promptly burst into tears of gratitude, that they had been spared this large financial outlay, however, Beauchamp queried, 'But you're already having alterations done for our accommodation here. Surely you don't want to be put to any more expense.'

'I shall be put to whatever expense I choose to. If I want to create you a flat and pay for the celebrations, then I shall do so, and you can either like it or lump it.'

After a few seconds of stunned silence, they both admitted that they would 'like it' very much, and were overwhelmed by her generosity.

'I've also spoken to one of our occasional maids, who is going to contact you about working regular hours here. I thought that would be a start in getting some more hands on deck for the amount of sheer hard labour you two have to get through. I'll see about a footman as soon as I can, then we can see how the land lies. Now, what "minor details" does that leave to be booked?'

'Photographer, car and chauffeur, bouquet, buttonholes; I could go on and on,' moaned Enid, in despair.

'Well, don't. Make a list and get some quotes, and we'll talk again. What about your honeymoon?'

'We were considering a week in the West Country,' admitted Enid.

'Is that all? But there's a big, wide world out there.' Lady A was scandalized, and even Hugo 'tut-tutted'.

'And the West Country's the small bit of it that we'd like to visit,' added Beauchamp.

'Are you absolutely sure? Because, money's no object, you know.'

'I know, your ladyship, but the most important thing is that we go exactly where we want to, and that happens to be the West Country, in this instance. We'll have the rest of our lives together to go exploring exotic destinations.'

'And I'm very fond of the books of Daphne du Maurier,' added Enid, unexpectedly.

'Well I'll be blowed! I've never even looked at them.' This was one occasion when Enid definitely had the upper hand over her benefactor. 'But you're not getting away with it that easily. Hugo and I will get a selection of holiday brochures and see if we can't possibly tempt you further afield.'

'That will be a waste of time, your ladyship,' Beauchamp informed her haughtily.

'Oh, I don't know. If we can't tempt you two, we may decide on a little trip ourselves, just to liven up our lives a little.'

In hearing this, Hugo made a strange face combining excitement with trepidation. He didn't trust Manda to choose somewhere where he might feel very uncomfortable, or where a revolution wouldn't break out the day after they arrived. He'd never really fancied going guerrilla-watching.

Saturday

The next morning, Lady Amanda scuttled along to the domestic quarters before breakfast had been served and bearded Beauchamp in his den. She needed the names of the occasional outdoor staff, so that they could plan their day. She'd already decided that they'd do the rounds of the travel agents in the morning to see if she and Hugo couldn't jazz up the honeymoon destination. In the afternoon they'd return home and carry out their interviews of the outdoor staff.

'You'll need their addresses, too,' Beauchamp advised her. 'Today is Saturday, and the men don't work weekends.'

'Why ever not?'

'Because it's not as if we're preparing for a garden party or fête; there's no goal date or urgency, so we let them work a five-day week. The job gets done, and the men are happier.

'Now, there are three of them that were working here when the bodies were found. Have you got a notebook and pen? You have? Right! You want to make a note of Edgar, Edmund, and Edward's details.'

'That could prove confusing,' remarked Lady A.

'Just a freak coincidence, your ladyship. Edgar Drake lives at 15 Twixt-the-Ways.'

'Never heard of it. Where the hell is it?'

'I'll give you precise directions after you've got all the necessary information, your ladyship. Edmund Darke lives at,' here he consulted his iPad again, he was a thoroughly modern manservant – '7, The Butts, and Edward Darle lives at 12A Scribes Street.'

'Well, that's me totally confused, and I thought I knew Belchester like the back of my hand,' declared Lady A, scribbling furiously to get down the last address before she forgot it.

'Now, directions.' Beauchamp cleared his throat and drew his eyebrows together in thought. 'You know the narrow lane that cuts between the shops on West Street, just a short way from the Market Cross on the right-hand side?'

Lady Amanda's face froze in contemplation of the exact location of this lane. 'Got it! Go on.'

'If you turn down there, that is Twixt-the-Ways itself. If you take the first left off it, where it bears to the right, you'll find yourself in The Butts, and if you just carry on down it instead of turning off, it runs into Scribes Street. In fact, The Butts joins Twixt-the-Ways and Scribes Street and is really not very long at all. They're all quite close together, and situated between the public gardens and the rear of the northern parade of shops.'

'Well I never. What a warren it must be round there, and I never knew these little back streets existed. It should be quite an adventure walking round there.'

'I could take you in the Rolls, but it might be a bit difficult negotiating such a large car in the very narrow lanes. I could, however, accompany you on foot, if you like?'

'I really don't think we shall need a bodyguard, Beauchamp. This is Belchester we're talking about, not Chicago.'

'As your ladyship insists,' the man agreed reluctantly. He wasn't at all happy about this. It was an area notorious for fights on a Saturday night, and some of the residents didn't always wait for dusk to start their alcoholic over-indulgence for the day.

Lady Amanda closed her notebook, shoved her pen behind her ear, and stumped off to the breakfast room to await her repast. She had planning to do; it was going to be a busy day.

On the way through the hall, she picked up Grandmama's silver-topped cane from the stick stand and rested it against the back of her chair, before sitting down and beginning to plot their programme of visits, starting with the location of the various travel agents' offices.

When Hugo entered the room, her thoughts were thoroughly disrupted. He'd discarded the pair of walking canes he had been using the day before and had reverted to his old Zimmer frame, which he had not used for ages.

'Hugo, is the pain really that bad?'

'I'll be OK once the jolly old pills take effect, then I can go back to my sticks.'

'Thank goodness for that. I'm supposed to be getting you mobile, not bedridden again. Now, whoever can that be at the door at this time of the morning?' she queried, as she heard the jangle of the pull bell in the portico. 'I expect Beauchamp will be along in a moment to tell us, when he brings in the victuals.'

On cue, a couple of minutes later, both Enid and Beauchamp appeared with the trolley of bacon, eggs, kidneys, etcetera, and the manservant informed them that the police must have released their tricycles, because the garage had just delivered them back, looking much better than they had before – in fact, they looked as good as new.

'How perfect, Hugo. If Beauchamp uses the estate Land Rover and trailer instead of the Rolls, he can drop us in the city centre with the tricycles, and yours has a little motor, so it won't be anywhere near as painful as having to walk, and we can affix our sticks on somehow for going into travel agencies and up and down garden paths.'

'But I haven't ridden for ages,' stated Hugo apprehensively.

'You'll soon get the hang of it again. It's as easy as falling off a bike ... or perhaps that wasn't quite appropriate – as easy as falling off a log.'

'But not with the same amount of bruising, I hope.' Hugo really did not sound enthusiastic. He'd never been over-fond of the vehicle allotted to him.

'Don't make a fuss. You'll love it once you get back in the saddle.'

'I'll print you out a little map from my computer and mark the three addresses on it with a highlighter pen,' offered Beauchamp.

'I didn't even know you had a computer,' said

Lady Amanda, surprised at this up-to-datedness that her manservant had begun to display, first with his iPad now with a computer. Whatever next?

'One has to keep up with modern technology, your ladyship, otherwise one gets left behind. I have even ordered a satellite navigation system for the Rolls, so we shall never get lost again.'

'Whatever is a satellite navigation system, Beauchamp?'

'It's a bit like you, your ladyship. It tells you where to go.' And he didn't even have a twitch of a smile as he said this.

Beauchamp was as good as his word, and printed off a map on which, not only the three addresses were marked, but all the travel agencies. There was no way he could dissuade his employer from looking for an exotic honeymoon destination, and at least the activity would keep both her and Hugo out of his hair for quite some time.

At the Market Cross in the city centre, he unloaded the tricycles from the trailer as the two oldsters struggled out of the Land Rover, then he strapped their sticks to their mode of transport, before driving off, extracting a promise from Lady A that she would call him on her mobile phone when they wanted picking up.

Hugo was rather wobbly with his steering at first, and slightly panicked when he first fired up his auxiliary motor, but he soon got the hang of it again, although Lady Amanda firmly believed that one lad, out walking a pair of miniature Dachshunds, would never be quite the same again after his encounter with Hugo at full thrust.

He overshot the first travel agency, having forgotten how hard he had to tug on the brakes, and that he had to turn off his engine, when he wanted to stop. Lady A rode serenely after him and shouted instructions until he'd managed to come to a complete halt, then supervised his about-turn.

Several travel agents and sundry members of their staff went off to lunch that day rather bemused at the visit they'd had from an ageing whirlwind with the enthusiasm of twenty, and an elderly man trying desperately to keep up with her, both physically and verbally.

At one o'clock she decided that they ought to call into an establishment that served food for lunch. This could be the start of their investigation of the eating places, on their hunt for Jimmy the Jemmy.

'But we haven't seen a picture of him, yet,' pleaded Hugo who, although hungry, didn't want to be challenged for staring at people as he ate. Getting involved in a 'are you lookin' at me, mate?' brawl was not his idea of fun.

'I'll know a convicted criminal when I see one,' declared Lady A with unquenchable confidence. 'Now, where shall we go?'

Belchester had a concentration of eating places to the north and south of East Street. There was a choice of a Chinese takeaway on Tobacco Road, a chip shop, Indian take-away and Italian restaurant actually on East Street, and The Cat and Footstool pub, which had its main doors on Beggars Road.

There were two other pubs to add to the

choice, The Clocky Hen next to the police station on South Street, and The Witches' Cauldron on West Street, and it was this latter that Lady Amanda decided was perfect.

'It's not just got the perfect location, just across the road from the entrance of Twixt-the-Ways, but I understand that that Jemmy person has actually been seen in there.'

Hugo wasn't so enthusiastic. The pub was known as having quite a rough clientele, and he was rather nervous, having been bullied at school. He could feel all the trepidation of the beginning of term flooding back through his body, a sensation he hadn't experienced since he was a teenager.

To be quite honest, he'd have been as full of trepidation, had she chosen The Clocky Hen. There was a similar slightly rough area behind that, contained in Lumpen Lane, Butts Ben, Moggs End, and Rag-a-Bone Road. It was certainly an area he wouldn't like to find himself in after dark, even with the pub being next door to the police station and the long arm of the law.

'Come along Hugo, stop dilly-dallying.' This shrill order brought him out of his miserable reverie, and it was with misgivings that he slowly dismounted from his tricycle. Lady A already had her stick out of its strap, and was tapping it on the ground with impatience. 'Now, which bar, Hugo? The public or the saloon?' she enquired.

'Definitely the saloon,' he replied, blanching at even the thought of what things would be like in the public bar. OK, so he was a coward and didn't like confrontation; so what? It was his life, and that was the way he liked things; nice and peaceful.

His braver companion threw open the door of the saloon bar and tootled, 'Good day, everyone. May we have a luncheon menu, please,' as she approached the bar. Hugo creeping along in her wake, looked terrified.

A hush fell over the whole bar, and all eyes turned to investigate whence this terribly upper-class voice had issued. If these were the clientele of the saloon bar, thought Hugo, trying to become invisible, then the public bar must be an even worse nightmare. Some customers weren't even wearing ties, and there wasn't a hat in sight, on either man or woman, not that there were many of the latter in here.

The barman hooked his thumb towards a blackboard on the wall which listed the food of the day, and asked, 'Are you lost or something, love?'

'No,' declared his new customer. 'I am neither lost, nor am I your love. I am merely hungry. I and my friend ... Hugo?' she called, having looked to her side, then behind her, and not found anyone she knew there. 'Where are you, Hugo?'

'Here, Manda,' came a hoarse whisper from the far side of a one-armed bandit.

'Well, get yourself over here and choose something from the food board, before I faint from lack of nourishment.'

She was disconcerted to hear this last phrase repeated in whispers around the bar, with some fair attempts at her accent. What was it with these people? 'And we'll have a couple of glasses of lemonade while we're waiting, if you'd be so kind, landlord.' Again, 'if you'd be so kind, landlord' was whispered round the bar like an echo.

Trying to ignore it, she gestured to Hugo to get to her side so that they could study the choices together. 'I think I'll have the fish and chips,' she declared, and Hugo was in full agreement.

'And mushy peas,' he augmented the order. It was these two words that did the rounds of the bar this time.

'And would you like a silver spoon with your ketchup?' asked the landlord, with a sarcastic leer.

'Absolutely not. I should prefer tartare sauce, and a spoon with that would be most useful.' Lady Amanda would not be intimidated. Hugo would, however, and cringed at this exchange. 'And we'll eat it over there,' she finally declared, pointing at an empty table in the furthermost corner. 'Bring our order over when it's ready.'

With that, she turned abruptly on her heel, ignoring the whispers of Madam La-Di-Da that followed her and a cowed Hugo across, to sit down. 'Not a bad little bar, if you ignore the customers,' she commented, while Hugo replied in a whisper,

'I'm absolutely terrified. What are we going to do if one of them tries to talk to us?'

'Make conversation,' she stated baldly, and sipped at her lemonade, which had just been placed on the table, her hand hardly displaying a tremor.

Chapter Nine

Hugo was so relieved to leave the pub that he accidentally passed wind as the door closed behind them, and a cheer went up from inside. Whether this was due to Hugo's unexpected social faux pas or because they'd left, neither could tell, but not a word was said about the incident.

Although they had been fed and watered, both of them felt a little achy about the joints and muscles as they set off for Twixt-the-Ways. Neither had taken exercise on the tricycles since well before Christmas, and the fact made itself known to both of them in the form of pain.

Luckily for them, 15 Twixt-the-Ways was not far down the lane. And it was with relief that they dismounted from the infernal machines and hobbled along the path to knock on the door, neither of them willing to discuss their lack of fitness or their age.

Their knock was answered by a man who looked totally unfit for manual work. He was even older than them, bent and twisted with age, his face a curtain of wrinkles, his hair, white as washing powder, but without the little blue speckles that particular substance seemed to sport these days.

'Mr Drake?' enquired Lady Amanda, hardly able to believe her eyes. 'Mr Edgar Drake?'

'Yes, ma'am. At your service. What can I do for you?'

'You've been working in the grounds of Belchester Towers?'

'That I have.' Here, the elderly man leaned towards his visitors and stared hard right into their faces. 'Why, it's your ladyship and Mr Chumley-umley-umple, if my eyes don't deceive me,' he declared in triumph.

Lady Amanda flashed Hugo one of her looks, which he took to be querying where this man kept his white stick and whether his guide dog attacked on command. Hugo himself looked utterly scandalised at this complete ruination of his family name. This was the man who should have been called Mangel, because he was certainly good at it.

'I wonder if we could come in for a few minutes, to talk about the recent deaths that have occurred up there?' asked her ladyship.

'Help yourself,' he invited them, turning aside and tripping over the doormat. Lady A put out a hand to catch him and helped him into his living room, delivering him safely to an armchair near the log fire. What on earth did this man do to earn his keep on the estate? He wasn't even capable of getting round his own home in safety.

'How well did you know Victor Mangel, the man who was found dead in the suit of armour?' she asked, feeling thoroughly dispirited.

'I didn't really know him at all. He worked on shrubs and trees, and I only saw him when he brought me clippings and such,' he replied, as if he was keeping a scrapbook rather than gardening, 'to burn,' he finished.

'Tell me, Mr Drake...'

'Do call me Ed. Everyone else does,' he entreated her, with a shy smile.

'Tell me, Ed, what exactly is it that you do on my estate?' She felt entitled to ask, as he seemed so unfit for any sort of physical activity that didn't involve braille.

'I'm responsible for bonfires. Always plenty to burn on an estate that size. I burns all the bits removed in the tidy-up,' he replied. 'I likes fire.' There was a dodgy statement, if ever she'd heard one, thought Lady Amanda. 'I have my little patch behind the stables, and everyone else brings me whatever they've removed or cut orf, be it branches, twigs or weeds,' he continued.

'I puts the weeds on to a special pile to dry them out and I burns all the dry stuff. Grass clippings go into a special pile for composting. We don't put the weeds in there in case they takes and grows, and blows their seeds all over the grounds,' he explained, suddenly becoming garrulous in his enthusiasm.

'Did you know either of the women who were killed?'

'No, yer ladyship. I has nothin' to do with the indoor staff, except sometimes I has a word with that Beecham fellah, if he's takin' the air, like.'

'Thank you very much, Mr ... Ed, and that's *Beauchamp,* if you want to pronounce his name correctly.'

'That's funny, yer ladyship; he told me the exact opposite. Well, you lives and learns. Good day to you both.'

The two visitors approached their tricycles to remount in quite a dejected manner. This visit had been a waste of both time and effort, and

Lady A resolved to speak to Evergreen about the quality of the casual staff he employed. The poor old chap they'd just visited wasn't really capable of anything, and she hated to think he was left in charge of bonfires. If things got out of hand, he could be responsible for the Great Fire of Belchester.

'He'll have to be let go with a small pension,' she declared, as she consulted the map Beauchamp had prepared for them, once again.

'Even I've got more go in me than that, and at least I can see where I'm going,' commented Hugo.

'OK,' said his companion, putting the map back in her coat pocket. 'If we turn left out of this property, then take the first left, we'll be in The Butts; then we need to look for number seven. Hi ho, Silver, and away!'

Her pedal-away wasn't quite so dramatic as her last words, but the thought was there, and Tonto was right behind her, head down, giving it all he had left which, admittedly, wasn't an awful lot.

Their next port of call was a well-cared-for cottage in a fairly derelict road. It had smart paintwork, and clean net curtains hung at the front window, through which issued the sound of a television at very high volume, broadcasting what sounded like sport.

Lady A rang the doorbell, but there was no response. She then knocked on the door, with similar results. Her next move was to ring the bell while simultaneously knocking at the door, to which she added a call of, 'Mr Darke. Mr Darke, you have visitors.'

There was still no response, so she beckoned Hugo to follow her round to the back. There was no point in showing her face at the window, as she would not be seen because of those sparkling net curtains.

Yes, just as she thought. The back door was unlocked. Without a twinge of guilt, she let herself in and headed for the front room, where she flung open the door and called loudly, 'Mr Darke? I've been knocking and ringing at the front door, but you didn't answer.'

The old man in the armchair looked up in surprise to see a stranger entering his living room, and grabbed the controller to turn down the television. 'I'm sorry,' he almost shouted. 'You'll have to speak up. I'm rather hard of hearing. And who the hell are you, bursting in on a man on a Saturday afternoon when he's trying to watch a bit of telly?'

'Lady Amanda Golightly: your employer,' she replied, fortissimo and with very exaggerated mouth movements. He obviously understood this, and he turned off the television and rose arthritically to his feet. 'How can I be of service, ma'am?' he enquired, actually tugging at a ratty forelock of iron-grey hair.

'Edmund Darke at your service, ma'am, but everyone calls me Edds, and I'd be honoured if you'd do the same.'

'Good afternoon, Edds. This is my friend Mr Cholmondley-Crichton-Crump, and we're looking into the recent tragic deaths at Belchester Towers. I wonder if you'd be good enough to tell me anything you know about poor Mr Mangel.'

All this time, Edmund Darke had had both of his hands cupped round his ears, to magnify any speech that came his way. He had obviously understood what was asked of him, because, with a smile of triumph, he replied, 'Arternoon, Mister Chumley-Critchy-Chump. Mangel be dead, you know. Found in a suit of armour 'e was.'

'We know that, Mr D ... Edds. I was wondering if you could tell us what sort of person he was.'

''E'd better 'earin' than me, that I can say, and 'e'd better sight than poor old Ed, and 'e were much spryer than old Eddie. Really, 'e were the fittest of all of us, exceptin' for Mr Evergreen oo's powerful fit!'

'What sort of person was he?'

''E were a terrible old gossip, that 'e were. 'E picked up anything 'e could and tittle-tattled it all over the estate, though I couldn't 'ear most of what 'e said, thank goodness. 'E were a bit of an old woman in that respect, and I don't 'ave time for stuff like that. 'Ad enough of that when my old woman were alive, if truth be told. Many's a time I'd just turn off my 'earin' aids if there were just 'im around, ma'am.'

'Thank you very much, er, Edds. You've been very frank with us,' shouted Lady A.

'Frank? No, don't know of no Frank workin' on the estate. Per'aps 'e's new and I 'aven't met 'im, yet.'

'No, there is no Frank.'

'I told you, I don't know no Frank, ma'am. You must've mis'eard me.'

'Did you know the two maids who died, Florrie

Searle and Edie Haire?'

'No, not at all. I kep' meself to the outdoors.'

'Thank you very much, Edds. You've been very 'elp ... er, helpful. Good day to you.' Lady Amanda didn't want to try to explain any further, as she could see a real conversational tangle looming on the horizon. 'Come along Hugo. We must get on.' Taking their leave politely was the easiest and most honourable way out.

Once outside, she sighed with relief. 'What a trial he must be to supervise on the job. I really don't understand what Evergreen thinks he's up to with the casual staff. One can hardly see his hand in front of his face, and the other couldn't hear a bomb go off, if it exploded just behind him. I wonder what our last candidate will be like.'

'Breathing would be good,' opined Hugo, waspishly.

'That's more than poor old Mangel is,' agreed Lady A, in an acid tone, pulling out her map once more, for a further consultation for directions.

'Right, if we go on down to the other end of this street and turn right at the T-junction, we'll be almost at one end of Scribes Street, although I don't know what end the numbers start. Then, afterwards, if we just go to the other end of it, it should take us to North Street, and we just need to call Beauchamp. We'll need to do that from the main road because he'd never get the Land Rover and trailer down these narrow thoroughfares.'

At the T-junction, they turned right and Lady A dismounted to see what number they were at. 'Just our luck – number a hundred and twenty-seven.'

'We'd have had to ride the whole length of the road anyway to get to North Street,' Hugo reminded her, 'so it doesn't really make any odds which end we're at. It's the same amount of pedalling, when you look at it.'

A short way up the road they stopped, when Hugo called out in apparent pain.

'Whatever's wrong, old stick?'

'I don't know. It's something round the back in a rather embarrassing place, and it hurts. Can you take a look? It feels like there's something sticking into me.'

Lady A marched round to the rear of Hugo's tricycle and doubled over with laughter. 'I say, old girl,' Hugo moaned, 'I don't see that my pain is any reason for mirth. What is it?'

'Hang on a mo',' she advised him, made a swift double-handed movement, then said, 'How does that feel?'

'Why, it's gone completely. Whatever did you do? Are you turning into some sort of psychic healer?'

'No, I just put your sticks back in their strap properly. They'd turned a bit, and were caught in the middle seam of your trousers. What you might call a bit of a "bummer".'

'Manda! Don't be so coarse! You've not been the same since Tabitha visited us,' he said for the second time, scandalised all over again.

'I know. She has that effect on me – always has – and it takes a while for it to wear off. I'll be all right in a couple of days, as long as she doesn't come back again.'

'I don't think there's any danger of that,' Hugo

assured her, as they set off on their last visit of the day.

12A Scribes Street was a Victorian terraced property with an overgrown garden and peeling paintwork, and didn't strike either of them as a likely home for an estate worker.

It took several knocks to bring anyone to the door, and, when the occupant opened it, they realised he was so slow because he was on crutches, having only one leg, the right limb ending just below the knee. Well, this really took the biscuit! Lady A would be having a very severe word with her head groundsman about the staff he had chosen to employ. How and why on earth had he given a job to a one-legged gardener?

'Mr Darle?' she enquired, hoping for a negative answer, and the information that Mr Darle was another occupant of the house altogether.

'Ah, your l-l-ladyship and M-m-mr Hugo. What an honour it is t-t-to find you on my d-d-d-doors-s-tep. Edward D-darle at your s-s-service, but please c-c-call m-me Eddie.'

Oh great. And he was a stutterer. It was like the three wise monkeys, only with old men: one couldn't see, one couldn't hear, and the third could barely speak. She'd have to get rid of them all, thought Lady Amanda, and do some interviewing herself, to make sure she got some fit men to undertake the work in the grounds. She'd give Evergreen a right flea in the ear when she caught up with him.

'Good afternoon, Eddie,' Hugo greeted him politely in the silence caused by his companion's furious thinking. 'We'd like to talk to you about the recent deaths at work. Can you tell us what you knew of Victor Mangel?'

'Sociable b-b-body, he was, always chatting and affable. I l-l-liked him. Real p-p-p-p-pity about what happened, although I d-d-don't understand exactly what that w-was.'

'The police are investigating, Eddie, as are we. We wondered if you'd heard or seen anything suspicious just before he disappeared?' This was easier going. The man might only have one leg and suffer from a stutter, but he seemed quite civilised.

'He w-w-was chattering on about something that he'd s-s-seen and was excited about, but I w-w-wasn't really listening. I was having trouble with my s-s-stump, if you'll p-pardon the expression, and the p-p-pain was d-distracting,' he replied, making them both start with excitement. Maybe they were on to something here.

'Could you just have a think and see if you can remember anything he said,' asked Lady A breathlessly.

There was silence for almost a minute, as Eddie scratched at his sparse hair, lost in recollection, then his face lit up. 'It was s-s-something to do with s-s-s ... s-s-s...' he ground to a halt with an expression of angry bewilderment on his face. He'd ground to a full stop, and would have to try a bump-start.

'S-s-s...' he tried again, but still couldn't get any further.

'Try a different letter,' advised Lady Amanda, who'd had a friend at school who'd stuttered and, sometimes, if she tried a word that began with a different letter of the alphabet, she could get underway again.

'It concerned a p-p-person,' – it had worked – 'he'd m-m-met and s-s-s ... s-s-s...' – but not for long. He'd come unstuck on the letter 's' again. With a frown of effort, his eyes nearly crossed, he tried again. 'A k-k-kind of c-c-caper.'

'What do you mean by "caper"?' asked Lady Amanda, now holding her breath with the tension of the situation.

'S-s-s ... s-s-s ... s-s-s...' Eddie turned dark red with his effort, then held up his hand. He'd done as much as he could. Grabbing a calendar from a small table in the hall, he pointed to the next day, and looked at them imploringly.

'We'll come back another day, but I can't guarantee tomorrow,' agreed Lady Amanda, understanding, but feeling utterly defeated. The door swung closed slowly, as Edward Darle retreated from the conversational battlefield, bloodied but unbowed.

As they tricycled away, Lady Amanda said, 'It sounds to me as if that Mangel fellow was involved in whatever happened while we were away. What do you think, Hugo?'

'I rather think you're right. Maybe this last one will remember something else overnight, if we're really lucky.'

'I just hope he doesn't try to phone us with what he's remembered,' declared her ladyship, her face all screwed up in a grimace of apprehension at the thought. 'We'll have to give Sergeant Glenister a ring straight away when we get in, to get him to come over with a picture of this Jemmy fellow, then we can get on with searching the watering holes of Belchester,' gabbled Lady A, swept away with excitement at the thought.

'Indeed,' agreed Hugo dourly, remembering the place where they'd taken lunch, and how intimidated he'd felt. 'I can't wait.' Again, he crossed his fingers at the untruth.

'Neither can I. And here we are, at the junction with North Street. What a silly I am. I could have phoned Beauchamp as soon as Eddie shut his door. He'd have been here by now. My brains must have been dulled by all that st-st-stuttering.'

'You bitch!' whispered Hugo under his breath, but very quietly, so there was no chance of his old friend hearing and verbally ripping his face off.

Chapter Ten

Once back in the house, Lady Amanda demanded a more substantial afternoon tea than normal, because of the amount of exercise she and Hugo had been forced to take, then got straight on the blower to Glenister, whose mobile phone number, fortunately, she possessed.

She was most surprised to hear a strident ringtone sounding from the next room, and when Glenister answered, he spoke before she had a chance to. 'If you're in the drawing room, I'll join you; I'm only in the next room.'

Beauchamp, who had not yet left the room, raised an eyebrow at her, and said, 'You never gave me a chance to tell you when you got back. You just went straight into your spiel about afternoon tea. If you'd just given me the opportunity, I'd have informed you he was already here.'

'How uppity you are this afternoon, Beauchamp,' she replied, blustering in her embarrassment. 'Well, be off with you and get on with the tea. The sooner you start it, the sooner I can satisfy my hunger, and you'd better make it for three, if Sergeant Glenister's here. I say, that blundering fool Moody isn't here as well, is he?'

'He has just left, your ladyship. Unfortunately for you, you have just missed him.' Beauchamp infused this statement with as much sarcasm as he could muster. 'Uppity' indeed! And who did she think she was, even if she was his employer? Oh, he genuinely *loved* working here. Just for that, he'd do her favourite anchovy toast. He almost whistled as he returned to the kitchen.

Sergeant Glenister entered the drawing room with a wide grin. 'Do you know, I still can't believe you ran into my uncle when you were in Scotland,' he opened. 'I hope he proved to be efficient.'

'He was a real pleasure to work with,' replied Lady A, 'but he had an absolute dope of a DC; not like here, where it was the other way round when we left. Congratulations, by the way, on your promotion, and your transfer to plain clothes.'

'Thank you very much,' the detective replied, as Hugo echoed these sentiments. 'If only Old Misery Guts could get another rank under his belt, they might move him to another division, but I'd probably have to make inspector first, so that's a long way off yet.'

'We'll do our best to help you on your way,' promised his hostess. 'In the meantime, we need to see a picture of this recently released Jemmy fellow, and I've ordered afternoon tea for three, if that suits you.'

'How very civilised of you,' replied Glenister, fumbling about in his inside jacket pocket.

'I'm so sorry about your clothes the other day. I'll reimburse you for any expense you've been put to,' offered Lady A with a smile, as she remembered what had happened to the inspector's face.

'And I'm sure you'll be glad to know that Inspector Moody is healing nicely,' he responded, handing her an A4 photocopy of a mug shot. 'You can keep that if you like. The original's in the office, so I can easily get another one.'

A slightly squeaky wheel announced the imminent arrival of the tea trolley, and Lady A's mouth began, very commonly, to water. She was absolutely starving, and couldn't believe her luck when the conveyance entered the room and she espied anchovy toast. And smoked salmon sandwiches. And a covered silver dish that proved to hold toasted teacakes, just dripping with melted butter. And, and, and, a plate of iced fondant fancies!

'Oh, Beauchamp!' she exclaimed, fighting the urge to dribble, 'You have really excelled yourself today.'

'I have anointed the smoked salmon sandwiches with horseradish mayonnaise, just as you like them, your ladyship,' he informed her, the tiniest hint of a smile at the sides of his mouth.

He knew she'd thought that, after she had spoken to him harshly and called him 'uppity', he would have produced an inferior repast, but that simply wasn't his way. She kept him on his toes, even if some of her criticism was unjustified.

He was a big boy now, and he could take it. Sticks and stones may break his bones, but words would never hurt him. And as long as he knew how to bite his tongue, things would never actually get to sticks and stones, and he'd be more than happy to see his days out here.

After they had partaken of tea and Detective Sergeant Glenister had taken his leave of them, she announced her intention of bearding Evergreen in his den, and asking him what the hell he was playing at, getting her to pay a decent wage to a bunch of unfit old men.

Hugo followed along behind her slowly, having reverted now to his trusty Zimmer frame. Lady A was still using a cane, so it wasn't as hard as it could have been to keep up, her still not being up to full speed. He was quite worried about the encounter that was about to happen, because Manda's temper had really risen, about the condition of the three people she paid to work in her grounds.

They found the head groundsman in the potting shed, planting seed trays for the annuals in late spring and summer. 'Good afternoon, Lady Amanda. How very civil of you to visit me at work,' he greeted her, with a smarmy smile.

'Evergreen,' she began, without preamble, 'I have visited, this afternoon, the three men you employ to help with the occasional garden clear-up – Ed, Edds, and Eddie, as I believe they are known to you.'

Evergreen's face slowly drained of colour and his grin turned into a grimace. 'I have observed,' his employer continued, 'that Mr Darke is virtually deaf, that Mr Drake certainly ought to be registered blind, and that Mr Darle has only one leg and suffers from a ferocious stutter that sometimes renders him, literally, speechless. What have you got to say for yourself?'

There was total silence in the potting shed.

Hugo cleared his throat in embarrassment, as she continued with, 'Well? How do you deem that they can be of any practical purpose in clearing the grounds?'

Evergreen was now a colour somewhere between crimson and purple, and began to bluster. 'I suppose I didn't really notice the deterioration in them over the years,' he tried first.

'Surely you noticed when Mr Darle came in one day with a leg missing?'

'He wore a prosthetic,' Evergreen defended himself.

'Did you not become aware of the fact that Mr Drake kept bumping into some things, and falling over others?'

'He works round behind the stables. I don't often have reason to go to where things are being burnt.'

'And that Mr Darke is unable to hear any of your orders. The man's practically stone deaf. What do you think you're playing at? You have taken advantage of my good nature for some perverse reason of your own.'

'I'm very sorry, your ladyship. Please don't give

me the elbow,' he pleaded.

'I can assure you that I shall not be offering you any part of my body. I shall, however, expect you to visit each of them tomorrow, in your own time, and tell them that I shall be paying them a small pension, and that their services are no longer required.

'I shall then expect you to put a note through the door of the local paper with an advertisement for casual gardeners, and a postcard to the same effect, in the windows of all the newsagents that still put such notices in their windows. And when we get applications for employment, I shall graciously allow you to sit in on *my* interviews with the candidates. Have you got that?'

'Yes, your ladyship. Thank you very much, your ladyship. You're too kind, your ladyship,' he burbled.

'Oh, don't gush, man. You'll make me sick. Just do your job as you're supposed to, and no more of this "hospital ward" stuff. I'm not a doctor, nor am I a charity, and, at the moment, you simply wouldn't believe how angry I am with you. Now buck up, man, and see if you can't give me a little value for money for a change.'

Lady A stumped out of the potting shed without the slightest need for her walking cane. It must have been the adrenaline coursing round her body that acted as a fully effective painkiller, and Hugo simply couldn't keep pace with her on the way back to the house.

'Come along, slowcoach,' she called over her shoulder, with no idea of the pace at which she was moving. 'For goodness sake get a move on,

Hugo, or you'll get moss and lichen growing on your north side.

'Now we've got that out of the way, I think we should hide ourselves away in the library and take a look at all the brochures we collected. I must say, I picked up some very esoteric ones that should provide very amusing reading.'

'You know they won't change their mind about their plans, don't you, Manda?'

'Of course I do, but it'll be fun to imagine the two of them in some of the more out of the way places in the literature I collected,' she replied, entering the library.

Hugo followed and sank gratefully into an armchair while Lady Amanda shared out the brochures, eventually spreading her selection out on a chesterfield before sinking down beside it.

After a few minutes of browsing, she called out, 'I've found some naturist holidays in this one. How do you think they'd take to that, Hugo?'

'Not their thing at all, I shouldn't say,' he replied.

'Enid's such a prude, I should think it would embarrass her just to see *herself* in a state of undress,' commented Lady Amanda.

'Hey, there are some holidays here where you can jump out of a helicopter on to the top of a mountain and ski down to the base,' Hugo chortled. 'That'd be a sight for sore eyes.'

'What about trekking in the jungle or canoeing down the Amazon? I say, can you imagine Enid's disgust if she found her legs covered in leeches?'

'She'd throw up on the spot.'

'And what about Beauchamp burned as red as

a beetroot?'

'That ought to ruffle his dignity,' replied Hugo.

'I say,' piped up Lady A. 'Do you think Beauchamp would wear gloves to put sun cream on Enid's back?' At this question, they both collapsed in *schadenfreudlich* laughter.

In such innocent pastimes they sat for more than an hour and a half, imagining Beauchamp and Enid in different inappropriate activities, before consigning their brochures to the waste bin and sighing in defeat. The West Country it would be, and nothing they could do would change their minds. All they could do was dream.

Although Lady Amanda had, reluctantly, agreed to be maid of honour – she could not be matron-of-honour, because she was an unmarried lady who was still 'unspoilt', and she was a bit old to be calling herself a bridesmaid – she was full of trepidation at the prospect. Good grief! What would she look like if Enid wanted her to wear one of those coloured meringue dresses?

The talk at dinner that evening was not all about the wedding, though. After the soup, she produced the photocopied mug shot that DS Glenister had given her and passed it across the table to Beauchamp and Enid. 'That, apparently,' she informed them, 'is Jimmy "the Jemmy" Aldridge, who has been sighted several times in Belchester.

'Tomorrow, Hugo and I will be taking every meal, with the exception of breakfast, in one of the eating places in Belchester, in the hope that we may spot him and put him under surveillance.'

'You'd better ask him to walk extra slowly, then.

The two of you aren't up to much,' commented Enid, then continued with, 'I don't half need a fag. I'm going outside; there's no need to wait for me.'

'Enid!' Lady A exploded, 'No matter how accurate your comment, I think that having nicotine in your system has played havoc with your manners.'

'I suggest you give me a call on the mobile, should you actually encounter him, and I will get to your location as quickly as I can,' offered Beauchamp, fortunately covering Enid's disgraceful reply of, 'Shove it, sister!'

That Night

Lady Amanda was so distracted by the thought of hunting for Jimmy the Jemmy that she found it difficult to sleep, and only managed to doze occasionally, spending most of her time under the covers tossing and turning with impatience for the morning to arrive.

At two o'clock, she gave up and got out of bed, put on her dressing gown, went downstairs and made a cup of tea. This she took back upstairs, and plonked herself down in the armchair that sat by her window.

Drawing back the curtains, she was surprised to see a dim light in the estate chapel. It had not been used in years and, as far as she knew, had been locked since before Papa died. Who on earth could be in there now? The light was not bright, and she made a guess that it was an oil lamp.

She was suddenly overcome by the overwhelming desire to wake Hugo and make sure she was not imagining things. Anyway, why should he be sleeping like a baby when she was absolutely wired?

Yes, she'd been right; Hugo proved to be out like a light, a small smile of contentment on his thoroughly relaxed features. 'Wake up, sleepy head,' she said in quite a loud voice, shaking him by the shoulder at the same time. At first, this produced only a couple of grunts and an enormous snore, but eventually, she managed to rouse him from what seemed to be near coma.

'Come on, you lazy old bear. I think there's something going on outside, and I need your opinion of it before I rouse Beauchamp, although it might be him, I suppose,' she said.

'What might be him?' Hugo was easier than usual to confuse due to his dozy state.

'I couldn't sleep, so I got a cup of tea and sat down to look out of the window. When I did, I noticed that there seemed to be a dim light on in the chapel and, to my knowledge, that place hasn't been used in years. Take a look and see what you think.'

Hugo dragged himself reluctantly from below the covers, pulled on his dressing gown sluggishly and hunted around for his slippers.

'Come on, you old tortoise, or it'll be breakfast time before you get to the window.'

'I'm going as fast as I can. Woman wakes up a man when he's having a lovely sleep just because she can't sleep, then expects him to be all bright-eyed and bushy-tailed. Just isn't on.'

'Stop whinging and get to that window, Hugo.'

Hugo finally pulled on his footwear and shuffled

over to the curtains, drawing them back reluctantly, then became galvanised by what he saw. 'I say, old girl, you're perfectly right. I can see a light, too, although it isn't very bright.'

'I wondered if maybe Beauchamp has had reason to go out there looking for something – it could be something quite odd, to do with the wedding, that we wouldn't guess in a million years.'

'I think,' suggested Hugo, confidently, 'that the best thing we could do would be to go to his room and see if he's there. If he's not, then everything's all right, and we can ask him about it in the morning.'

'Excellent idea, Hugo.'

Beauchamp, however, was found to be fast asleep in his bed, lying as tidily as he conducted himself during daylight hours. There was not even a hint of a snore, and even his hair was perfectly in place. Had they not known him and been aware of the rise and fall of his chest, they might assume him to be dead.

'Wake up, Beauchamp, please,' implored Hugo in a very polite voice. Beauchamp did not stir. 'I say, old chap, would you mind waking up?' he continued, while squeezing the manservant's hand.

'Stir your stumps, sleepy head,' roared Lady Amanda, abandoning manners and agitating the man's feet through the covers. 'There's mischief afoot.'

'Wha … what's going on?' asked Beauchamp, suddenly upright, his eyes wide open, his coiffure still unruffled.

'There's a light in the old chapel. We thought at first it was you, but it obviously isn't, so we need to investigate.'

Beauchamp's bedroom was on the same side of the house, but a floor higher, so they should get a decent view from his window and, when they looked, there was more to see. The main low light had been extinguished, but a brighter smaller light was mobile inside it. 'There's definitely someone in there,' opined Lady A, 'and he's changed to a torch now.'

'Should we go down and challenge him?' asked Hugo, with trepidation.

'Not on your nelly,' replied Beauchamp, making an uncharacteristic jaunt into the vernacular.

'The torch has been switched off,' Lady A announced, her nose firmly pressed against the window pane.

'Look! There's someone outside the chapel,' hissed Hugo, excitedly. 'I can just see his shape.'

'We mustn't go down there until the morning. It's too dangerous. One of us might get injured, or even killed. If it's who we think it is, there've been three deaths already, and he might be armed.' Beauchamp was saying no more than common sense dictated, as he reached into the top drawer of his tallboy and extracted a pair of binoculars.

'You cunning old fox, Beauchamp,' crowed Lady A with admiration. 'Can you actually see who it is?'

'Not from this distance with any accuracy but, in the main, it doesn't look unlike that photograph you showed us at dinner,' he replied. 'Damn! He's gone round the other side, but he's at least had the decency to lock the door.'

'Where on earth did he get the keys from?'

Lady Amanda was horrified.

'If someone gained access to the house while we were all away, they could have got into my key cupboard by picking the lock, and had all the keys copied before we came back.' Beauchamp was very glum.

'We need to change all the locks,' declared Lady A. 'Get on to a locksmith first thing in the morning, and arrange for it to be done as soon as possible. In the meantime, you must ring the ironmonger's and order bolts for all the exterior doors that don't have them, until the locksmith has been.

'He won't dare come into the house when it's occupied; the bolts are just in case.' She blustered to a halt, afraid she might have revealed her inner coward, not often acknowledged, but she didn't fancy being attacked in her bed totally out of the blue.

Chapter Eleven

Sunday

Lady Amanda shocked herself by sleeping like an old dog for the rest of the night, and Enid had to shake her awake for her early morning tea, which she didn't bring up until nine o'clock, after Beauchamp told her what had happened during the night.

She awoke with a shock, throwing her hands in

the air and calling out, 'I have learnt karate, you know. You won't get away with this.'

'It's only me, Amanda, with your morning cuppa. Beauchamp's been over to the chapel, and is waiting to go back over there when you and Mr Hugo are ready.'

'Well, tell him not to do any breakfast for us. There's a greasy spoon café to the east side of Belchester, and we'll have a full English there, see if we can spot this Jemmy character. He's got to eat somewhere and that seems like a likely place to start. I couldn't stop thinking about it when I first went to bed.'

'Very well, dear. As you like. I shall be outside having a gasper if you need me,' she finished, turned on her heel, and exited like an addict facing imminent cold turkey.

'I must get that woman some patches,' thought the occupant of the bed, downing her tea in one and making a grab for her clothes, preparatory to yelling Hugo out from under his bed clothes and into his day clothes.

A few minutes later, a stentorian voice could be heard coming from Mr Cholmondley-Crichton-Crump's room. 'COME ALONG NOW, HUGO. DOWN THE HATCH IN ONE WITH THAT TEA. GET ON WITH IT, MAN. WHAT? YOU'RE GOING INTO THE BATHROOM TO GET DRESSED? YOU OLD WOMAN. YOU HAVEN'T GOT ANYTHING I HAVEN'T SEEN BEFORE.'

Lady Amanda stopped at that point, remembering his extreme modesty when he had been trying on new underwear, and realising that, as a maiden lady and only child who had led a very sheltered life, he did have quite a lot with which she was not acquainted, and she had no desire to be educated in that department at this time of the morning, or, in fact, at any time of any day.

She showed her unspoken gratitude to his modesty by being extra nice to him when he emerged from the bathroom, somewhat sketchily dressed, but in quite good time. 'Come along, old chap. We're going out for breakfast. But we'll take a look in that chapel before we go,' she almost cooed at him.

Startled at this change of plan, as well as mood, Hugo's first question was a stark, 'Where?' They were supposed to be eating breakfast at home.

'That greasy spoon café over on Station Road. If chummy was here last night – "the Jemmy", not you, Hugo,' – for Hugo used to be called Chummy on occasion in the past – 'he might eat breakfast there to celebrate whatever he was up to. Or, he might just go there for breakfast anyway.'

'What's the place called?' was his second question.

'Um ... The Greasy Spoon,' replied Lady A, feeling rather foolish.

'Fascinating. How quaint and original.' Hugo had recovered sufficiently to add a tiny pinch of sarcasm to his voice.

Beauchamp heard them arrive in the hall and immediately appeared through the green baize door, ready to accompany them to the chapel, a large key in his right hand. 'Enid's already outside,' he informed them.

'Having a fag. I know,' Lady A interrupted him.

'...so we can set straight off,' he continued,

without comment. 'She delivered your message about breakfast.'

'Let's get sleuthing, then.' Her ladyship was much braver in daylight and in company, when she knew the chapel had been deserted and locked up. 'I'm really up for this.'

The chapel had been ignored for many a year and had become rather like a horror-film set. Cobwebs were draped all over the place, a thick layer of dust covered everything, and the once bright stained-glass windows were filthy with dirt.

The few hymn and service books that had long dwelt here had been badly chewed by rodents, and there was the scuffle of tiny clawed feet behind the wainscoting and even under the altar, the covers of which hung in discoloured tatters, their grandeur long gone in decay.

Some of the kneelers also showed signs of having been light snacks for little creatures, and the scurry of myriad insects was almost audible, so many of them were there.

The lady from the town who used to come in to clean the brasses – now long deceased – would have been scandalised to see the state of her previous living attention, and the silver had been put in the bank when her father died.

There were commemorative plaques everywhere, some stone and some brass, memorials to long-dead members of the Golightly family. Lady A's ancestor who had built the place originally had even been arrogantly vain enough to erect some to family members who had died long before the chapel was built, to give it a bit of 'history and class' in his opinion.

Light filtered in fitfully through the filthy windows, making some random patches of colour on the stone floor, illuminating, here and there, little piles of rodent dropping, and other delicacies of neglect.

The Sanctuary light no longer burnt.

It was to this scene that, Beauchamp having turned the key in the lock, four figures now entered, their eyes straining through the gloom to discern anything out of place. Until recently, the place had been exactly as it had been left when it was locked up and forsaken, but now there was a surfeit of unsuitable ornamentation in its secret shelter.

'OhmyGod!' (An exclamation made one word with the sense of shock.)

'Great heavens above!'

'Crikey!'

'Bloody hell!'

Thus, the four expressed their feelings on suddenly seeing what had been stashed under the sacred roof. There, on top of the altar, was the silver plate that had been filched from the butler's pantry. There, on the front pews, were the collections of Meissen and Worcester. There, on the choir pews, were the trophies, cups and shields that had disappeared from the billiard room.

There, in fact, somewhere in the body of the small chapel, was everything that had been stolen from Belchester Towers over the last week or two, including some items that had not even been missed.

'Goodness gracious me!' cried Lady Amanda, as

she stared at what adorned the top of a small oak table at the rear of the building, originally there to hold leaflets about the history of the Golightly family, now sadly all consumed by the present occupants of the building, who had left not a paragraph or a sentence behind for posterity.

'My silver bibelots!' she cried. 'I'd never even missed them. It shows you how often I go into my boudoir.'

'My only Charles Horner hatpin is there, too,' Enid croaked, her voice now hoarse with cigarette smoke. 'I'll deck the bastard if I ever find him.' Lady Amanda was too shocked to chide her for her language.

'And my silver cufflinks,' added Beauchamp, astonished that he had not noticed the loss.

'And my gold cufflinks and dress studs, plus my father's pocket watch,' concluded Hugo. 'He has had a thorough rifle through our stuff, hasn't he? And that's since we've been back, because I had the cufflinks and studs with me in Scotland.'

There was such a silence as to allow the scufflings of mice and other small mammals to reach their ears, and help raise goose-bumps and give them the chills, as they digested the fact that the thief had been in the house since they had returned to it and that there had, at times, maybe been only the thickness of a wall between them and the imminent danger he represented.

'I'm going to lock all this lot away, your ladyship, and I suggest we go back to the house for a strong cup of sweet tea. Do you want me to inform Inspector Moody?'

'Absolutely not!' exclaimed Lady A with fervour. 'This is personal, and we'll sort it out ourselves. We'll be ready tonight for when I'm sure he'll return.'

'As your ladyship wishes.'

'I'm going for another fag.' Enid was getting totally predictable, as are of course, all addicts, thought Lady Amanda with a total lack of understanding.

The plan for the day's nourishment was to take breakfast in the café, then lunch in The Cat and Footstool on Beggars Road, and dinner in The Clocky Hen, right down at the bottom of South Street, from where they would telephone Beauchamp to pick up them and their tricycles, and ferry them back home.

He was able to drop them in Station Road, right outside The Greasy Spoon, which was nearly full at this time of day with men in donkey jackets, even on a Sunday. Employers no longer had any respect for the Sabbath. No doubt, in the summer, the uniform of choice was string vests, thought Lady A rather loftily, but came down to earth with a bump when she caught sight of the man behind the counter.

He wore a filthy apron over a washed-out rugby shirt and ancient jeans. His hair was an indeterminate colour and hadn't seen a barber's scissors or shampoo for some time. The most striking thing about him, however, was his right eye. Where the black centre was normally located was a white blank; obviously he was blind in this eye.

And to prove this beyond a doubt, he wore a pair of glasses which had a lens only in the space for the left eye. Where the lens for the right eye should have been located, was just an empty space, which he disconcertingly put his finger through to rub his itchy eyelid.

'What can I get you an' the wife, mate?' the man enquired of Hugo, who was too nervous to put him right. He didn't want to get into an argument in a place full of men in donkey jackets.

'Do you do a full fry-up?' he enquired timidly.

'Course we do, squire. Why do you think this place is called The Greasy Spoon? That's our speciality. In fact we do an all-day breakfast for people who keep irregular hours. Two? And do you want a mug o' char with that?'

Not really understanding what a mug o' char was, Hugo thought it best to agree, and turned to find them a table, as Lady A asked him, 'Have you ordered?'

'I think so,' he replied, hope in his voice.

'I can't see anyone in here that looks like chummy, can you?' she asked, as they sat down at a recently vacated table.

'Not yet,' replied Hugo, who had kept his eyes to himself since they'd entered, as he didn't fancy them turning black as a result of unwelcome curiosity. 'I haven't had the chance to have a good look round yet.'

'Well, get your peepers swivelling. I've thought about lunchtime yesterday, and I also don't remember anyone who looked like him in The Witches' Cauldron, but we're doing the next three most likely places today. If nothing comes of it, we can always put The Witches' Cauldron back in the mix.'

Hugo didn't hear most of this as, at the mere mention of the previous lunchtime's visit to the pub, he had broken out in a sweat of fear. 'Hugo, are you listening to me?' asked his breakfast companion, crossly.

'No,' he replied, totally throwing her off balance.

'What do you mean, no? Why on earth not?'

'Because places like this make me feel I'm going to decorate my underpants in a very childish way.'

'Really?' This was a reaction that would never have crossed Lady Amanda's mind, and she found it novel as well as disgusting. 'Well, just don't do it. Here comes our breakfast.'

Hugo shovelled down his food and slurped his tea like the most ill-bred navvy, then rose immediately to leave. 'You settle up. I'll meet you outside,' he whispered hoarsely, looking from side to side as if for an assassin.

'OK, Hugo. Just calm down. I'll be out in a minute,' Lady A replied, looking at him as if he had gone mad.

Hugo bolted out of the door as if all the hounds of hell were after him, only to find that he had jumped from the frying pan into the fire. Two unshaven men with bald heads who had settled up and left just before him, were examining the tricycles with rapt fascination.

'This belong to you?' one of them rasped, a look in his eyes that Hugo could not read.

'Yes,' he squeaked, his voice as high-pitched as a girl's. He harboured the terrible fear that they would beat him up, then steal the tricycles. They looked so rough and tough that he felt his sphincter contract and twitch with terror.

They were both looking at him, now, probably deciding where to dump his body when they'd finished with him. Oh God, what was he going to do? Where was Manda? How had he found himself in this ghastly situation?

One of the men spoke; the rougher-looking, more muscular one, but Hugo was so paralysed with fear that he didn't hear what he said. Repeating himself, the man asked, 'Would you mind if I had a ride of your tricycle? I've never seen one this big before. I'll only take it down to the junction with Cathedral Avenue and back.'

Hugo nearly fainted with relief, and nodded as the other man asked, 'Me, too?' and wasn't even intimidated when Manda came out of the café and asked, in quite an angry voice, where the hell their tricycles had gone.

They passed an hour in the cathedral, then walked down North Street wheeling their vehicles, so that they could do some window shopping. There was time to pass before they could contemplate ordering lunch, and it had to be filled somehow.

Bumping into Sir Jolyon and Lady Felicity ffolliat DeWinter just outside the Market Cross gave them an excuse to seek this structure's shelter and sit on a bench for half an hour or so, to pass a little more time in catching up with gossip about mutual friends, and the murder trial for which a date had just been set.

By the time they'd had a good old exchange of news, Lady A judged it late enough for them to head for The Cat and Footstool, and they parted from their acquaintances, remounted their tricycles, and headed off down East Street. They turned right into Beggars Run and found the pub just off the junction on their right.

Chaining their vehicles to fence posts in the car park, they surveyed the public house, which neither of them had visited before. It looked slightly more respectable than yesterday's example of a local hostelry, and they approached it with a mixture of hope and trepidation.

Without a word, they both headed for the door marked 'Saloon Bar', knowing that they would have to brave a quick visit to the public bar at some point, because it was possible that this was where Jimmy the Jemmy would feel more at home, given his recent accommodation at Her Majesty's pleasure.

Their shepherd's pie was acceptable, but their mission proved fruitless and, having made two lemonades last two and a half hours, they were ushered out of the pub by the landlord at closing time, this being an establishment that had not applied for an all-day licence.

The Clocky Hen was a different story altogether. They had gone into the library to spend a couple of hours reading the day's newspapers until it was opening time, then cycled to their final destination.

At first it seemed to be full of off-duty police officers, being next to the police station, but Lady A wasn't fooled by that. She led Hugo reluctantly into the public bar, thinking of the advice to keep one's friends close, and one's enemies even closer.

Where better for Jimmy the Jemmy to hang out than next to the police station. They'd never think to look for him there, and he probably thought he'd be safe as houses, right under their noses. But then, he had Lady A to deal with now, having crossed her severely.

She'd run the gamut of saucy and impudent looks and ordered two Virgin Marys when her eye was caught by a particularly loud tweed jacket, and she nearly fainted clean away when she looked upwards and was absolutely convinced that she had spotted her man. That face looked very familiar.

As unobtrusively as possible, she pointed out the figure to Hugo who agreed that he did, indeed, look extremely familiar. 'In that case,' she said in a hoarse whisper, 'I'm going to slip next door and see if I can raise DS Glenister to come in and arrest him. You keep a sharp eye on him while I'm gone. Don't let him get away. And pay for our drinks while you're at it. I need to be off quickly in case he rumbles us and makes a break for it.'

She bustled out of the exit and Hugo was left to juggle a pocketful of change and watch their target who didn't, at least at the moment, appear to be off anywhere.

Lady Amanda, meanwhile, rushed into the police station and up to the desk, asking officiously if she could see DS Glenister, as it was of vital importance in the solving of several serious crimes. The officer on duty took exception to her superior manner, and replied, with some satisfaction, that DS Glenister was not on duty at the moment, but he'd call another officer to look after her.

'As long as he's CID and not of inferior rank,' she trumpeted at the man, looking down her nose, so filled was she with self-importance. The duty officer made a quick call on an internal telephone and Lady A was just pumping herself up to be at her upper-class best, when Inspector Moody hove into view through the double swing doors.

'What do you want?' were his opening and far from encouraging words.

'This officer is summoning somebody to deal with me,' she informed him in a superior manner that was matchless.

'I know,' he replied, exasperated. 'Why do you think I'm here? It's me he summoned, you silly old dear.'

'Don't you talk to me like that when I've gone and found Jimmy the Jemmy for you, and left my friend Hugo guarding him so that he doesn't escape.'

'You never have!' exclaimed Moody in disbelief.

'Come with me and I'll show you,' she declared, in triumph.

Back in the pub. Hugo saw the door open and his friend enter the bar with Moody in tow, just as chummy put his empty glass on the bar and headed for the rear exit. He had to do something, and do it fast, before the criminal got away.

Hugo moved across the intervening space as quickly as he could, caught hold of the man's jacket sleeve and said, 'I am making a citizen's arrest. I know who you are and the police are on the way.'

By this time, Lady A had spotted him with her quarry, and was blundering through the other drinkers, like a galleon in full sail, with Moody in her wake. When she finally got to Hugo and his prisoner, she said, 'Here is your man, Detective Inspector Moody. I recognised his face as familiar as soon as we entered the bar. He's been hiding here, right under your nose, all this time.'

Inspector Moody's face broke out into a grin of absolute glee as he said, 'May I introduce you, once again, to PC Spouph. You obviously misidentified him, with him not being in uniform.'

Hugo's hand fell to his side, and his face fell almost as far, as he realised what fools they had made of themselves.

'What?' spluttered Lady Amanda.

'He's one of my uniformed officers who was in attendance in your own home when one of the maids was murdered. Don't you remember?'

Chapter Twelve

That Night

It had taken several cocktails to assuage Lady A's embarrassment at what had happened earlier in The Clocky Hen, and it was only now, after several of Beauchamp's finest efforts, that she could contemplate the future with anything but shame.

'Buck up, your ladyship. Remember we're going to keep surveillance on the old chapel tonight, to see if we can't catch a rat in our trap. If I can lock him in, I can push hard on the key so that he can't get his in from the other side while you dial 999.' Beauchamp had evidently been giving the evening's activities some thought.

'I shay,' she said, her voice rather louder than was necessary, 'that'sh a jolly good id-id-idea.' Lady Amanda's speech had become rather slushy as she 'relaxed' rather more than necessary.

'Manda, I do believe you're tiddly,' observed Hugo, with a slightly squiffy smile himself, for he had partaken of just as many cocktails as his friend, and then giggled.

'Oh dear,' remarked Beauchamp, as he observed the elderly pair. 'Things may get rather trickier than I had anticipated.'

'I've only had two drinky-winkies,' brayed Lady Amanda.

'Me too,' agreed Hugo over-vehemently.

'You've had two Hammer Horrors and two Lawnmowers apiece – two different cocktails but two of each, making four, if my maths is not mistaken,' Beauchamp reminded them.

'That must be why I need a little snoozy-woozy.' Lady Amanda yawned extravagantly and swayed a little on her feet.

'But, your ladyship, due to your late return from Belchester, we've actually stayed up, so that we don't have to get ready for bed and get up again, before we go out on surveillance. It's half-past one, and we said we'd go outside at two o'clock, which is the time you saw the lights in the chapel last night.' Beauchamp feared she was going to blow their plans completely.

'Well, I'm going to need my frame,' whined Hugo. 'I'm never steady on my feet late at night.'

'And with a bellyful of booze,' muttered the manservant under his breath.

'I want a frame too. Find one for me, Beauchy-Weaushy.' Lady Amanda had become like a petulant child while under the influence.

Beauchy-Weaushy obligingly set off to fetch Hugo's Zimmer plus one more, so that they could get their clandestine activities over and done with, and he could offload these two into the land of nod. But before that, he was going to pour one more liquid down their throats that might actually help the situation.

When he returned, he left the two frames outside the door and entered to see the squiffy pair trying to walk. 'Sit down again,' he ordered them quite sternly. 'I'm going to make a pot of Beauchamp's Infallible Remedy for you, to set you up for the adventure to come.'

He returned from the kitchen some minutes later and found them both dozing on a sofa, like a pair of bookends. 'Wakey, wakey!' he called in a stentorian voice that made them both jerk awake with surprise. 'Beauchamp's Infallible Remedy has arrived.'

'Oh, goody goody,' trilled Lady A, rubbing her hands together.

'Yummy,' said Hugo, doing the same, although neither of them had any idea of the ingredients.

Beauchamp had purposely made no mention of the fact that it was non-alcoholic, and usually used as a remedy to counteract drunkenness. He had brought it along in a silver pot, and its recipe was two parts espresso coffee to two parts cocoa, with two spoonfuls of sugar to each serving, to be served hot. The final touch was a sprinkle of cinnamon on the top of each serving, the powder for which resided in a small silver bowl on the tray next to the Limoges coffee cans and saucers.

It was a recipe he had learned from his mother, which she had used on Lady A's father, when he got himself rather tired and emotional in his mistress's presence, and, although it wasn't alcoholic, it sure packed a punch, and had been known to fool the uninitiated.

Both Hugo and Lady Amanda were fooled by its potency, and lapped it up eagerly, both asking, to Beauchamp's delight, for a second helping. His fiancée wasn't so easily fooled.

'I'm going outside for a fag,' Enid informed whoever could be bothered to listen, putting her cup back on the tray in disgust. 'I'll meet you at the door.'

Beauchamp rolled his eyes at nobody in particular as he walked down the hall, and began to gird his loins for a very difficult, if not dangerous, evening.

When he managed to herd the two unruly old hooligans outside, Lady A was singing 'On Mother Kelly's Doorstep', and Hugo was whistling 'In a Monastery Garden', a blissful smile on his face. It didn't seem to matter too much at the moment, because there were no lights on in the chapel, but Beauchamp, nevertheless, did his best to shut them up in case there was someone out of their sightline.

'Enid, for heaven's sake don't light another cigarette,' he ordered in a harsh undertone.

'Why ever not? Smoking's not noisy,' Enid protested, her packet already out of her pocket.

'Because of the smell of the smoke,' he explained.

'But they always smoke when they're on surveillance in films and on the telly,' his fiancée protested.

'Which shows that it's all "let's pretend". If our villain was over by the chapel right now, but out of sight, and he lit a cigarette, we should smell it and immediately be able to pinpoint his position.' Beauchamp always found that a 'f'r-instance' quite often helped where no explanation would prove as effective.

'I see what you mean,' agreed Enid, realisation dawning on her, as she slipped the cardboard packet away again. 'Good thinking!'

This exchange had allowed his two elderly charges to get away from him and, as he turned round to continue guiding them, he spotted them much further ahead, but separated by quite a distance, and taking an inexplicably curvy route.

They looked just like a couple of giant snails ambling across the lawn in the moonlight, their course completely haphazard. He had not realised that one could still execute a drunken gait with a Zimmer frame.

Beauchamp urgently pointed Enid in the direction of Hugo, whom she found singing under his breath, some nursery song about ten thousand men and some royal or other. 'Hush, Mr Hugo,' she urged him in low tones. 'There might be a murderer concealed near us.'

'Sorry! Sorry! Shhh!' he replied, this last with a finger unsteadily at his lips to indicate silence.

Beauchamp headed after Lady Amanda, whom

he found in a condition he would not have thought possible. 'Bloody bastard!' she was muttering. 'Bloody thieving, murdering bastard! Murdering scum! Bloody criminal shitbag! Steal my stuff would you? Kill my staff would you? Well we'll just see about that!'

'Hush, your ladyship. The miscreant could be anywhere within earshot but out of sight. You don't want him to hear you, do you?'

'Want to sodding kill him!' she declared.

'Hush!' Beauchamp chided her. 'How can we sneak upon him if he can hear us coming? We'll never catch him if you carry on like this. He'll hear us coming and get clean away.'

'Good point, my man. Good point. Hush up, or you'll give away our position, whispering in that loud voice.'

The manservant was happy to have the blame shifted to him, if it shut her ladyship's mouth and stopped her cursing and swearing. Turning her towards the chapel, he took her arm and began guiding her, in silence now, towards their goal.

He had reconnected the electricity supply to the building during the day, and popped over to see that it was still working, and that the wires had not been chewed by small animals, but there was not even the glow of an oil lamp or the beam of a torch to be seen in the building tonight.

That could mean one of two things: either the miscreant had already been and gone, or he had not yet arrived. If it was the former, he would probably have left some tell-tale sign by having moved something that would give him away. Heaven knew, there were enough things in there to start an antique shop. If he hadn't been there yet, he didn't know what they'd do. He'd just have to play it by ear.

Inserting the key in the lock, he noted that it would not turn widdershins. That could mean only one thing. He turned the key clockwise, and it clicked. He was right! The chapel had been left unlocked, and he knew he'd locked it when he'd come over here much earlier. He must have already been.

Unlocking the door again, he flung it open boldly, confident that there was no one inside, and put his left hand to the wall just inside the doorway to put on the lights. What this revealed was almost unbelievable, and he was wrong in his last supposition.

That 'they' had already been was evident from the fact that not one stick of the contraband loot they had found there the night before remained in evidence, but the building wasn't quite deserted of people.

Splayed across the altar, like an offering at a ceremony of human sacrifice, was the body of Evergreen, and he was as dead as dead could be, a knife sticking up from his chest making him appear to be like a character in a murder weekend, and somehow unreal.

Lady Amanda nearly went arse-over-tit in her hurry to get down the aisle and make a closer inspection. As she waddled, driving her Zimmer before her, she could be heard to mutter, 'My head groundsman! My bloody head groundsman! Murdered! The bastard! He's going to bloody well pay for this!'

Hugo, who had not heard her cursing before, exclaimed in shock and horror, 'Manda! Mind your language! That's disgraceful!'

'I know,' she replied, only catching his last two words, 'and my bloody head groundsman, too!'

'I meant your language,' replied Hugo, scandalised all over again – *déjà vu* with foul language.

'You're only saying that because you won't have to bloody well find another one, as well as two maids and four f**king casual outdoor staff. Sodding hell, what a pickle I'm in on the domestic front. F**k it all!'

At this point, Beauchamp lost his rag for the first time that the household could remember, grabbed his employer's walking frame, and threw it aside as if it had been made of paper – not a particularly spectacular feat, of course, when one thinks that the things are only aluminium, and weigh virtually nothing. The real surprise was that he flung it with such anger that it landed at the other end of the pew.

He then put one hand round her mouth, managing to smother an exclamation of '*shi–*', as Lady A realised what was happening to her. He grabbed her under her pendulous breasts with the other arm, and pulled her backwards off her feet, all the fight seemed to go out of her, and she hung there like a rag doll.

As he dragged Lady A back down the aisle, he called out to Enid. 'The door key's in my right hand pocket. I didn't leave it in the door in case someone came along and locked us in. Take it, then get Mr Hugo, lock up this place, and get him back to the house and into his bed.'

'Aye aye, Cap'n!' Enid was on board, and in action mode.

'I'll phone the police, once I've got this drunken old biddy back into her cage,' were his last words before he left the building.

Moody may have been furious to be roused from bed for a second time, but he had no idea how lucky he had been the previous evening, when the residents of Belchester Towers had not informed him of the fact that they had discovered all the stolen goods from the robberies.

He stamped round the bedroom, cursing as he got dressed, thoroughly waking his long-suffering wife, but not matching the level of language that Lady Amanda had sunk to, had he but known it. His body did contain one bone of consideration, however, even if it was the smallest one his skeleton possessed, and he did not turn on the light as he dressed.

He met Glenister at the station, as they lived in opposite directions, and they proceeded out of the tiny city, north towards their target. 'I can't believe there's a fourth dead body on the property. Is one of those mad old nobs a serial killer?' asked Moody, still very tetchy, as he considered where he was going – yet again!

'I hardly think so, sir,' replied Glenister, showing just a smidgen of logic as he added, 'The first murder took place while they were all away in Scotland, and the place was locked up, to all intents and purposes.'

'Picky, picky, Sergeant. Perhaps the old dear got a helicopter for Christmas. If she'd had access to one of those up there, she could have got down here, committed the murder, and been back in her bed in Scotland, before morning.' Moody was trying as hard as he could to make this fantastic theory stick.

'You're presuming that she has already got a helicopter pilot's licence, and that she arranged the lessons and the test before acquiring this enormously expensive flying machine? And there'd been absolutely no gossip about what she was up to, even up to the present day? Here, where you can't blow your nose without someone being aware of it on the other side of the city.'

Moody fell silent, completely defeated, but whatever happened, he was determined to try to pin everything that had occurred at Belchester Towers on to its owner, if it was the last thing he did.

Beauchamp met them at the front door, crumblies now tidily disposed of, and looked the two detectives up and down. 'Good wee small hours to you,' he greeted them, inventively. Glenister looked as tidy as he did on a call in more sociable hours; Moody, not so. His tie was erratically knotted, his top shirt button undone, his knitted tank top on inside out, and he sported one other sartorial faux pas which Beauchamp couldn't resist mentioning as he took their coats.

'Nice pair of shoes,' he said in his most polite voice. 'I'd be willing to bet you've got another pair just like it at home.'

Detective Inspector Moody looked down slowly, genuinely concerned about what he was about to see. Damn and blast it! He'd put on one black lace-up and one brown, and all because he didn't turn on the blasted light in case it disturbed his wife too much. Well it wouldn't happen again. He'd put a hundred watt bulb in the ceiling light fitting and see how she liked that when he was called out during the hours of darkness. He wasn't being caught out like this again.

Beauchamp retreated to the cloakroom with their outer garments, mouthing, 'Gotcha!'

Enid was in the hall when he returned, and the inspector was looking around him as if in search of something. 'Can I be of assistance, Inspector,' Beauchamp offered, wondering what it was he sought.

'Where're Lady Muck and Little Lord Fauntleroy? I'd have expected them to be waiting for us when we arrived.'

'I'm afraid they're asleep, sir,' replied the manservant, with a small smile of satisfaction on his face.

'Well, go and wake them, then,' ordered Moody.

'I can't,' replied Beauchamp, baldly.

'Why not?' asked the inspector, testily.

'Because they're blind drunk,' was the reply he received. 'So you'll have to deal with just Mrs Tweedie and I for now. You are, of course, welcome to come back tomorrow when they are sober to interview them, but I expect their memories of tonight will be very hazy.'

If Moody had been a dog, he would have been growling in a threatening manner by now, and seriously considering biting. 'Then you had better conduct me to where you found the body, hadn't you?' His words came out through gritted teeth, while Glenister found it hard to suppress a gleeful grin, and had to conjure up a pretend cough, so that he could put his hand over his mouth to disguise this fact.

As they walked across the moonlit grass, Moody told Beauchamp that he really should be grateful to the Belchester Constabulary. Although they had been the victims of several crimes, he reckoned many more had been averted. 'PC Spouph informed me that he made a check of the outside of the house and grounds every couple of days while you were away.'

'It didn't seem to do much good, did it? Maybe he only sloped off up here for a secret smoke in uniform,' replied Beauchamp, slightly surprised at such enthusiasm above and beyond the call of duty.

'Spouph is a very conscientious officer in his attention to detail, where his job is concerned. He wants to progress within the force, so he works hard.'

'A most admirable trait. Why is he not with you tonight?'

'There was no need, at this preliminary stage, to include a uniformed officer. So, this is the chapel,' he declared, stating the bleedin' obvious, in the manservant's opinion. 'I've never been in here before.'

'It's been out of use for years, sir. I have the key, if you'll excuse me.' Beauchamp opened the door, leaned in to switch on the lights, then stood aside so that they could precede him into the interior.

When they had entered, Moody asked a little frostily, 'So, where is this body supposed to be, then?'

'It's on the altar. Can't you see...' Beauchamp's voice trailed into silence as he entered the chapel and looked to the far end of the aisle where the altar, quite obviously, had nothing but dust and the remains of a tattered altar cloth on it.

'But it was spread lengthwise along the altar with a damned great knife sticking out of its chest, and it was definitely Evergreen the head groundsman. We all saw it. We all identified him.'

'What, two drunks who didn't know what way was up, a menopausal widow, and you, so distracted by your charges that you'd be willing to bear witness to pink elephants if your employer said she'd seen them?' Moody, triumphant, was not a pretty sight.

'I'm not having this!' Beauchamp was as furious again, as he had been with Lady Amanda earlier, and he marched purposefully down the aisle to examine the altar close-up. 'There!' he cried, in a voice of conviction. 'You get yourself up here, Detective Inspector. This altar cloth, which has obviously been on this altar for decades, has bloodstains on it: not very large ones, but fresh ones, nevertheless.'

Moody reluctantly took his mismatched shoes for a short walk, and had to agree that there were indeed areas of discolouration that looked remarkably like blood, on what remained of the altar cloth. 'But we'll have to get forensics to confirm that. It might not be blood, let alone human. It might represent the last mark made by a rodent that had been involved in a fight and mortally injured.'

'Thank you very much, Mr Grimm. You should have started that story with "Once upon a time..."' snapped Beauchamp.

'How dare you, you jumped-up little domestic!' Moody was furious at being thus addressed.

'I dare to, because I was here earlier with three other witnesses, when there was the dead body of the head groundsman draped across that altar. It may be gone now, but it was there then, and when I present you with evidence of that fact, you decide it's just the remains of a bit of a punch-up between a couple of mice. Now, get out of her ladyship's chapel before I throw you out!'

Discretion being the better part of valour, Moody 'got', with Glenister in his wake, chuckling as quietly as he could at his boss's humiliation.

Chapter Thirteen

Monday

Oh, God! Whatever had happened last night to make her head thump so, and her stomach churn like an angry sea. Lady Amanda became aware of daylight filtering through her slightly open eyelids and closed them again as tightly as she could. She felt like she had been charged by an elephant, but had no recollection of the event.

A quick survey of her body parts informed her

that, if she was not mistaken, she had bruised her posterior during whatever the incident had been, and she wished that either Enid or Beauchamp would arrive with early morning tea, to explain everything to her.

A quick glance at her bedside clock to ascertain the hour, informed her that it was half-past-eleven, and she shot upright with disbelief, an action which resulted in a howl of pain which sounded not unlike that of a wolf.

A high-pitched scream from elsewhere in the house seemed to suggest that, whatever it was that had happened, Hugo had been similarly involved, and probably felt as wretched as did she, although she couldn't be sure about the bruising.

The door slid slowly open to reveal Enid with a cup and saucer in her hand, a look of sympathy on her face. 'How are you feeling?' she asked, as she entered and approached the bed.

'Stop shouting,' whispered Lady Amanda, who was a little sensitive to sound at the moment. 'What happened?'

'You went on a bit of a bender last night,' whispered Enid.

'Did I disgrace myself?'

'You did, rather.'

'Oh, bog! I don't want to know about it yet. Tell me one more thing, though. Did Hugo do the same?'

'He certainly went on a bender.'

'But he didn't disgrace himself?'

'No.'

'How galling. Thank you for the tea. My tongue's like a sheet of sandpaper. I'll be down as soon as I'm capable of walking.'

'Would you like me to stay and help you dress?'

'Yes, please; I would, actually.'

Enid sat down on the end of the bed, taking care not to shake the mattress too much.

In Hugo's room, as the echoes of his scream died away, he sat in his bed with his head between his hands, hardly able to believe that there weren't little men inside it with jackhammers, working away like billy-o – and probably all wearing donkey jackets, to boot.

Beauchamp insinuated himself into the room soundlessly, and approached the bed, similarly bearing morning refreshment. 'Good morning, Mr Hugo,' he whispered, being rather more used to dealing with hangovers than Enid. His fiancée's late husband, after all, had been teetotal, but Beauchamp himself had of course worked for Lady Amanda's parents, both of whom could put it away like good 'uns.

'Beauch...' Hugo never got any further than the first syllable of the manservant's name: the first syllable felt like the volume of it had lifted the top of his head from his skull.

'Don't talk, Mr Hugo. I'll explain everything to you, and you just drink your tea. I expect you're very thirsty.' Beauchamp's voice had dropped to a whisper. Hugo began to nod his head, then desisted after the first movement. It was just too painful to complete the indication of agreement.

'You and Lady Amanda had decided to stay up and beard the criminal in the chapel, if and when he returned, in the night.' Thus far, Hugo was okay. It was shortly after that that things became a little fuzzy.

'Then the two of you,' Beauchamp continued, trying to keep a straight face, 'went on a bit of a toot, and you both got rather squiffy.'

'I can remember feeling rather light-headed, and something chocolaty – maybe even a cup of coffee – then, I'm afraid, the old memory box is completely empty. The next thing I was conscious of was waking up a short while ago, feeling as if I'd been run down by a speeding lorry. Have I missed much?'

'Rather a lot, I'm afraid. Would you like me to fill you in on the details?' asked Hugo's visitor.

'I didn't do anything awful, did I?'

'Not beyond a bit of singing and whistling.'

'Did Manda? Do anything awful, that is?'

'Rather,' replied Beauchamp, with complete candour, thinking back to Lady Amanda's rambunctious drunken behaviour.

'Chocks away, then,' ordered Hugo, cheering up considerably at this news.

Everyone was silent at breakfast, which was more like brunch, given the time it was. Lady Amanda sat with her head bowed, but when she looked at Hugo, she found he was smiling a secret smile.

'You know, don't you?' she challenged him.

'Know what?' he replied, trying to look innocent of any knowledge whatsoever.

'You do, don't you? Well, I don't want to be told just yet, unless there's anything that I absolutely need to be made aware of,' she replied.

It was Beauchamp who spoke. 'I'm sorry to inform you, if you don't remember that Evergreen's dead – murdered – and that, since last night, his body has disappeared.' At this bit of news of something that had occurred after he had been carted off to bed, Hugo's mouth fell open in surprise.

'And all the stolen goods that had been in the chapel had disappeared,' concluded the manservant in a further effort to jog their memories, calmly buttering a piece of toast. 'Inspector Moody and his sergeant have already called here while you two were sleeping it off, and will be returning today with a forensics team.

'It may gladden your heart to know that the detective inspector turned up here wearing mismatched shoes,' Beauchamp concluded, thus raising a small smile from both Lady A and Hugo, before silence, once more, held sway in the room.

After they had eaten and much coffee had been drunk, Enid shooed them both off to bed for a nap, promising to call them when the police arrived.

This occurred at just a minute past two o'clock, and very frustrated indeed was Detective Inspector Moody at his supposed witnesses' lack of memory of anything that had happened the previous night. He was also very disconcerted by the way that both of them kept glancing down at his shoes and smiling. Beauchamp had evidently blabbed about his sartorial faux pas, the rat-fink.

'I did a bit of singing and whistling,' offered Hugo as some sort of consolation.

'But I remember absolutely nothing since we had cocktails.

'And, apparently, I was drunk to the wide,' Lady

Amanda informed him, almost with pride, now that she had got used to the idea, but had not yet learnt the details of what had actually occurred.

'I simply can't believe that you remember nothing whatsoever,' protested Moody, moodily, living up to his name.

'If you want to know what I got up to, you will have to ask Beauchamp and Enid. They were sober. I, unfortunately, had so many cocktails, that they produced a state of alcoholic amnesia about which there is nothing I can do.'

'In that case, I should like to speak to both of your staff, to ascertain exactly what you did do last night. In the meantime, I have a team of officers on their way here to search every nook, cranny and corner, to see if they can't discover the whereabouts of the body that your staff claim has gone walkabout.'

'And Hugo and I shall be going out,' Lady A stated, much to Hugo's surprise.

'Where are we going, Manda?' he asked, more than ready just to go back to bed, and not get up again until the next day.

'Come with me, and I shall tell you,' she replied, not wishing to give anything away to the inspector. 'I shall need your services later, Beauchamp. Please let me know when you are free.'

In fact, so impatient was she to be off and out, that she was waiting in the hall when both detectives appeared through the baize door, Moody doubled over with laughter, and Glenister having a good chuckle. Lady A sighed. She wasn't looking forward to learning what Beauchamp had evidently just divulged to them, about her forgotten antics of the night before.

She was, however, looking forward to her little afternoon jaunt. There was a town about ten miles to the north-west, just at the foot of the gently rolling hills that led inland, that was as picturesque as a film set; a rival, in fact, to Belchester's charms. Its main street was a steep slope that reduced older cars to first gear, lined with the most beautiful historic buildings which had, over the years, been converted to shops, banks and teashops.

It was also the location of the 'later' nineteenth-century fake castle where Tabitha's friend lived, and she thought she might just pop in to say hello while they were over there. It couldn't do any harm to widen the circle of her acquaintances, and would give her someone else to bore with her stories about how old her property was.

Many of the commercial establishments were now antique shops which proved, with the proximity of a river and a beautiful park with a boating lake, a magnet to tourists, especially those from the United States, and the shopkeepers were in price-ticket heaven with the freedom to exaggerate with which this endowed them.

Lady A was convinced that if the goods had been taken away to be passed through a 'fence', then this was the place that would provide the obvious target for placing items. She intended that Beauchamp could drive them over there, and they would investigate the shops in the guise of a couple of bumbling old twits with more money than sense, but who had a sharp idea of what they wanted to buy – i.e. what had been stolen.

Beauchamp dropped them at the very top of the hill that was the High Street, and reminded them to call him when they were ready to be picked up, and as he drove off, Lady A rubbed her hands again, in gleeful anticipation of what they might find on the shelves of the town's antique establishments. Hugo was more concerned with not losing his footing – he was still feeling a little unsteady and had brought sticks – and bowling down the hill like a human ball.

But, before anything else, Lady A insisted that they call at the main entrance to the castle, which was situated at the very top of the hill, and had been rebuilt in real fairy-tale style. It would not be too much of a trial to see the Draycott-Bayliss family again.

She pulled at the old-fashioned iron bell-pull with a sneer, but only because it was bigger than, and seemed to be more ancient, than her own. Within seconds the door was opened by an impeccably attired footman, right down to his white gloves.

'I wonder if we may see Mr and Mrs Draycott-Bayliss. This gentleman's sister is an old school-friend of Mrs Draycott-Bayliss, and they visited my establishment with their daughter Daisy recently.'

'Poppy,' hissed Hugo, as the footman's face creased in pain at this mis-naming of the daughter of the family.

'Poppy, I mean. So many girls are named after flowers these days that it can become really confusing. Do, please, excuse my lapse of memory.'

The footman asked if she had a calling card and proffered a small silver tray on which she could place it. Fumbling around in her capacious handbag, Lady A did eventually find an old dog-eared card from years gone by, and put it down with a deprecating smile.

Without another word, the footman turned and walked away towards a door down the hall to the right, that was standing slightly ajar, and through which could be heard the sound of husband and wife laughing over something which had tickled their sense of humour.

He returned almost immediately, empty-handed and informed the visitors that Sir and Madam were not at home at the moment, but that he had retained the visiting card for them for when they returned, and firmly closed the door in their faces.

'Blasted cheek!' exclaimed Lady Amanda, as they walked away from the crenellations and actual portcullis. 'We could hear very well that they were at home. I bet that cow Tabitha has phoned her up and blackened my name because of the way things happened before she packed up in a huff and left.'

'Well, you were in a rather foul mood all the time she was with us.'

'And no wonder, with those hairy hooligans of hers. She should have taken them straight to a cattery before she arrived at Belchester Towers. They were not suitable to be part of her luggage.' And that was the end of that. They set off down the hill, both walking very carefully, lest the slope should be their undoing and the bringer of skinned knees and bruised dignities.

The first shop they arrived at seemed to be filled more with junk than antiques, and did not take long to discount as a possible target for the stolen property. As it was near the top of the hill, though, this was not surprising, as the main bus stop and parking was at the foot of the hill, and a lot of tourists probably never made it this far up the street, before lack of oxygen from the sheer altitude discouraged them from going any further.

As they descended, so the quality of the goods on offer and the prices ascended, the latter faster than the former. This prolonged the time they spent in each shop as, not only did they have to look out for anything that had come from Belchester Towers, but Lady A found herself enchanted with some of the pieces for sale.

In the sixth shop, just off the main drag and down a pretty side street, she fell in love with a silver stirrup cup, and before Hugo knew it was happening, she had whipped out her debit card and bought it, asking the proprietor to hang on to it until her man came in to collect it later.

Two shops later, he had to literally drag her away from what he considered an awfully tacky musical compact that had completely won her heart, at a ridiculously inflated price. 'Manda, it's only base metal, the enamelling on the front is really second rate, and he wants two hundred pounds for it. I didn't think you were the sort of person who would let yourself be so openly rooked.'

'But I love it, Hugo,' she pleaded.

'Then ask Beauchamp to look for one on the Internet when we get home. This chap charges like a raging bull.' She'd forget about it as soon as she left the shop, so Hugo had no cause for real concern.

With this dangled carrot, she reluctantly let herself be led back to the pavement and into the shop next door, so prolific was this type of establishment in this town, that they were often side by side.

Inside, another crisis arose. 'Manda, I know it's pretty, but do you really need an ivory and ebony sewing box. Do you really *need* it?'

'*Want* it, Hugo. *Want* it,' she replied sulkily, hugging the *objet* in question to her chest, as if to demonstrate proprietorial rights.

'But it's seven hundred and fifty pounds. Isn't that rather excessive when you've just spent a small fortune on a solid silver stirrup cup?'

'No! *Want* it. My man, could you wrap this for me, please?' she summoned the shop owner imperiously, while snubbing Hugo's financial caution at the same time.

Hugo couldn't take this without a small fight. 'You're only buying these things because you were snubbed at the castle. Isn't over a thousand pounds a bit steep for being cut by someone you've only ever met once, and who's Tabitha's friend and not yours?'

'Shush, Hugo!' Lady A chided him, for she did not want it to get around that she'd been rebuffed by the town's castle-keeper. 'I just fancied a bit of a splurge, that's all. You know I love pretty things. I may have a surfeit at Belchester Towers, but there's nothing to say I can't fancy something new to look at.' That should settle his hash.

'I think we should call Beauchamp, now,' suggested Hugo, suddenly aware that he didn't want to go into any more shops with his friend, lest she spend even more money, and beginning to feel desperate. He knew she had been robbed, but her home was stuffed with fine and valuable objects. She needed more like a desert needed an extra bucket of sand.

Watching the man lovingly wrap her purchase – no doubt thinking of the huge profit he was making – she nodded almost absent-mindedly, so enchanted was she with her find, and Hugo made the necessary telephone call. 'And do hurry, old chap. She's spending.'

'Tell him not to hurry,' Lady A interrupted. 'I fancy a cup of tea in one of these delicious tea-shops with which the town seems so amply supplied.'

Sighing, Hugo passed on this piece of information, said he'd phone again when they'd done so, and followed her into an establishment where everything in the furniture realm seemed to be drowning in gingham.

Seating herself at one of these checked horrors of tables, his friend smiled wolfishly and ordered a pot of jasmine tea with a dangerous twinkle in her eye that warned Hugo that something was afoot, and he knew he wasn't going to like it, whatever it was.

When Hugo telephoned again, Beauchamp literally ran outside to the Rolls, his face a mask of panic at how much his employer might have spent.

Chapter Fourteen

'I'm going to set a trap for him,' announced Lady Amanda that evening.

'For whom?' asked Beauchamp, with impeccable grammar.

'With what?' asked Enid, simultaneously.

Hugo merely dozed in his armchair, replete after a much-needed dinner, given that they had only eaten brunch that day.

'For that Jimmy the Jemmy, thief and murderer,' she replied to Beauchamp. Turning her head towards Enid, she informed her, 'With my jewellery.' A further head movement produced, in a louder voice, 'Hugo! Wake up! I'm laying a trap.'

'Whaa...? Whassup?' Hugo re-joined them, mentally in a somewhat fuddled state.

'I'm planning to set a trap for that felon using my jewellery, and I shall need your help.'

'Howzat?'

'I want you and I to go for a walk in the grounds talking loudly about how I've put all my good jewels in my boudoir as they're to go off to be cleaned first thing in the morning, and I don't want to be disturbed too early.

'I also want Beauchamp and you, Enid, to go outside and have a walk around in a different part of the grounds, also having an indiscreet conversation about how worried you are that my gems are to be left out overnight, unguarded, and not locked away as they usually are.'

'Why?' Hugo had still not caught on to her plans.

'The miscreant is quite evidently hiding out somewhere about the property, as he seems to know everything that goes on. Last night he seemed to know that we were going back to the chapel, and removed all the evidence, and left the body of Evergreen there as a warning to us.'

'Which you're not going to heed?'

'Absolutely not!'

'Which will put all of us in danger?'

'Four against one, Hugo.'

'What if he's got a gang?'

'What if he's got a verruca?'

'What if he's got a gun?'

'Grow a backbone, Hugo!'

'I'll only go if I can take one of your father's guns.'

'How very un-English of you.'

'How very sensible of me. That's the deal. Take it or leave it.'

'Very well. But I'm very disappointed in you.'

'It's better than being very sorry for me, that I'm dead.'

'True.'

'I suggest we all go armed in some way. The man's killed four times,' interjected Beauchamp, proving that he was probably the only grown-up present. Enid had gone outside for a cigarette, as usual.

Lady Amanda and Hugo went outside very soon after this conversation, Lady Amanda with a small pistol in her handbag, Hugo with one in his jacket pocket, both now feeling rather foolish. Hugo had ascertained that they would have to take turns in watching the jewels through the long hours of the night. If he could get this blasted inconvenient bit of baiting over with, he could get to bed sooner and, at least, get *some* sleep before he had to take his turn on watch.

'I don't think I'm taking any risk at all,' brayed Lady A in loud tones as they walked slowly round the lawned area between the house and chapel. 'After taking all that swag,' – Hugo blushed at her use of such a corny word – 'last night, and doing away with Evergreen, I think he's probably left the area by now.'

'Really?' asked Hugo, equally loudly, and playing along merely for form's sake.

'He'll probably be a couple of counties away by now, if not completely out of the country. Pastures new – that's what he'll be after, with the lot he's copped from here.'

They continued to maunder on in this 'am-dram' way for half an hour, and it proved quite a strain on the imagination. Finally, with relief, they headed back indoors and sent Beauchamp and Enid out to walk around the area to the rear of the house near the stables, to conduct a conversation of similar drivel.

'Do you think that villain's still hanging around?' asked Enid, remembering to use her most timid voice, as she dragged hungrily on her Benson & Hedges. She found the nicotine in her system made her bold, and she needed to sound vulnerable, in case the murdering thief was listening.

'I shouldn't think so. I reckon he'll be long gone,' replied Beauchamp manfully, trying not to cough from the smoke that was blowing round his head. He hoped that Enid was going to give up her filthy habit before they got married. She was a totally different person with this insidious drug in her blood steam.

'I do hope you're right,' continued his fiancée, 'as she's going to be leaving all that nearly priceless collection of jewellery out of the safe tonight. If she'd only arranged for it to be picked up later in the day, there'd be no need to expose it to danger like that in her boudoir.'

'Quite right, Enid, my dear, but I don't think there's any danger of it being stolen almost from under her nose.'

Thirty minutes and four cigarettes later, they too returned to the house, to find Lady Amanda had gone upstairs to sort through her jewels and make a decision as to which pieces she would use to bait her trap.

'What about the emerald necklace?' they heard her ask Hugo as they approached the room.

'Much too valuable,' he declared vehemently. 'You know how difficult it is to find a decent emerald, and how much they cost. How many are there in that necklace? And they're all over a carat; some much bigger.'

'I didn't know you were such a connoisseur of gemstones, Hugo. But I have to use the big pieces. Small-fry wouldn't be worth his while.'

'But he wouldn't know that until he'd already broken in and we'd nabbed him.'

'In fact,' Beauchamp's voice sounded, as he and Enid entered the room, 'you don't really have to leave out any jewellery at all. How would he know the difference?'

Lady Amanda immediately rummaged around in her bedside table and produced a notepad and pencil. After holding a forefinger up to her lips to silence them she wrote, then displayed the message, 'He may have bugged the place while we were away. He could be listening to us now'.

The other three looked surprised at the thought, but no one had the temerity to suggest that she was exaggerating the situation, and nodded solemnly at her, as she put the emeralds back in its locking case.

'I'm only going to leave out the most expensive ones that really need cleaning,' she said, while extracting some truly awful strings of plastic and glass beads from a bedside cabinet. 'It's not worth it having the cheaper stuff cleaned, as I hardly wear it.'

'Just so, your ladyship,' agreed Beauchamp, with a conspiratorial wink. 'What absolutely fabulous diamonds there are in that tiara.'

Suddenly catching on, Enid added, 'And the sapphires in that necklace and bracelet are out of this world,' as Lady Amanda added a truly awful plastic brooch of a cat to the pile of useless junk she had produced, to represent the finest of her adornments.

'Thank you all so much for your compliments. I have been well provided for by my forebears. And now we must discuss the insurance claim for what has been stolen recently.'

On their way downstairs, Beauchamp leant unusually close to his employer and whispered into her ear, 'A stroke of genius to mention the insurance claim. If he was listening, he'll think we've given up all hope of getting back anything he took.'

They adjourned to the staff bathroom and turned on all the taps, as they had seen done in films. If someone had bugged the house, this was supposed to prevent them being able to hear any conversation, as the noise of the water would obliterate it.

'It's my room, so I'll take first watch,' volunteered Lady A. 'We should each do two hours, by my reckoning, to cover the hours when we would all be asleep.'

'Huh!' Hugo felt very disgruntled. 'If you take first watch, then you don't have to have your sleep disturbed at all. You just go to bed a little later. Well, I want last watch, so that it just seems that I've got up at sparrow-fart.'

Beauchamp sighed with resignation. 'OK, Enid and I will take the two middle watches.'

'If we did them together, we could play cards for four hours,' said Enid, suddenly seeing a bright side.

'I say, you're right. We could always catch up our sleep with a nap during the day,' replied Beauchamp, in total agreement. 'Right then, that's settled. What time will you go on guard duty, your ladyship?'

'When we turn out the lights. Shall we say about ten?'

'Hey, that means I have to get up at four

o'clock. Have a heart! At least make it eleven,' pleaded Hugo.

'Fair enough, Huggy-Wuggy.' Lady Amanda addressed her friend thus out of sheer excitement.

'Manda! Really!' Hugo admonished her.

'Cocktail time, Beauchamp.'

'As long as you don't take too many tonight. We don't want a repetition of last night, now, do we?' was that manservant's advice, as he made for the door, Enid on his heels.

'Tell me what I did last night, Hugo. I still don't know.'

Hugo obliged, and when Beauchamp returned with his laden tray, she refused one of the already mixed drinks and asked him if he'd be so kind as to rustle her up a Virgin Mary.

Lady Amanda entered her boudoir a little after eleven o'clock in her dressing gown and slippers, and armed with her library book, a plate of biscuits, a torch, and a flask of cocoa. That lot should keep her going for two hours, no trouble.

She poured herself a cup of cocoa, put her flask, cup, and plate on a side-table, and lay down on the chaise longue to read. She was about a third of the way through a very fast-paced thriller, and was eager to get on with the plot.

As she read, she shivered slightly. As an extra incentive to the thief, the sash window had been left open just a tiny bit, advertising that he would not have to work too hard to get at his target.

Slipping quickly back into her bedroom, she grabbed the eiderdown from the top of the bed, and rushed back to settle down, once more, on the chaise longue. The pile of junk jewellery was still where she had left it, and the human hair affixed with saliva (Enid and Beauchamp's, respectively, of course) across the door of her safe was still in place. All was well. It was early yet, though.

Her book was really hotting up now; the author was racking up the tension. She must get more out from the library by this writer. The storyline was absolutely riveting.

The next sensation of which she was aware was of a hand gently shaking her shoulder, and she opened her eyes to see Beauchamp sitting on the chaise longue beside her. 'I thought I'd better wake you,' he said. 'I've been sitting here for fifteen minutes, but you were well away.'

'I wasn't sleeping,' she objected.

'I'm afraid you were, and you were snoring as well,' he countered.

'Absolute nonsense,' she refuted.

'True. Completely true.' Enid's voice came from behind her, over by the window. She had forgotten that these two would be keeping a double watch together.

They were really into their card games, and the time simply flew by for them, a table lamp giving enough light for them to see by. At a quarter-to-six, well after the appointed time for their relief, Beauchamp made a short trip to Hugo's room to find that his alarm clock had indeed, rung, but he had slept right through its urgent summons and was still peacefully sleeping like a baby.

With infinite mercy, and respect for the man's age, the manservant crept his way out again, and he and Enid had another hour of card games.

The man would be very apologetic when he awoke to find he had missed his stint on guard duty, but at his age, the sleep would do him much more good.

Chapter Fifteen

Tuesday

The next morning, Beauchamp was almost jumping with excitement, and could hardly contain himself. He was acting like a child waiting for permission to open his Christmas presents.

'Whatever is the matter with you? Do you need to go to the little boys' room?' Lady Amanda asked. She was feeling rather grumpy, having done her guard duty the night before, when Hugo had been left to sleep through his, and the thief had failed to show at all, after all their plotting and effort.

'I've just remembered something my mother told me that was before my time, but may explain a lot of things that have happened lately,' he told her, almost hopping up and down. 'And we can investigate after breakfast.'

'Investigate what?' she asked, now intrigued.

'Spill the beans, old man,' instructed Hugo, glad to have someone to take the heat away from his dereliction of duty.

'This all happened before the war,' he began. 'Your father was always a – how can I put it without sounding really insulting – shall we say that he was a less than honest man?'

'I think that's fair,' agreed Lady A.

'And he definitely saw the approach of war as a retail opportunity, albeit a black-market one. Before hostilities broke out, he brought a team of labourers down from London and had them dig out the floor of one of the stables, explaining that he wanted somewhere to store his valuables from the house, should there be air raids in the area, because of the harbour nearby.

'They knew no better, not being local, excavated it, then built a substantial cellar for him. He fed them and provided them with beer to keep them from going into the town and talking about what they were doing, even though it sounded innocent enough.

'A little knowledge is a dangerous thing, and he knew that it could be his undoing if anyone in Belchester found out what he was up to. They could put two and two together as well as anyone else, and they knew his character.

'When war broke out and there were shortages, that cellar was full of black market gear, as well as illegally distilled spirits and weapons. Your father had a really black heart.'

'Huh!' retorted Lady Amanda. 'That's the pot calling the kettle black.'

'That's as may be, but that stables cellar is probably still there, and I'd put my shirt on the premise that the whole lot of the stolen items are now stored, away from open sight, there. This Jemmy must somehow have gleaned information from one of the original labourers – maybe he's a son or grandson of one of them. I can't think of any other way he might have found out,' declared the manservant.

'I'd bet my blouse that Evergreen knew about it. He's been here since the Ark.'

'He was probably in on it,' suggested Beauchamp, getting even more excited. 'That's why he kept the others on despite their decrepitude. He could get away with a lot more with those three around than with someone more alert.'

'That must have been why he was killed,' interjected Hugo.

'I'm going outside for a fag,' said Enid.

When they reached the stable block, Beauchamp was not sure which stable the cellar had been situated in, and there were quite a lot of them. A closer inspection confirmed that, while there were now no horses in residence, nobody had cleared out all the old straw and quite a lot of 'do-dos' from when they were used. The floors were invisible.

'We'll need to split up and use brooms,' declared Beauchamp, turning on his heel and marching back towards the house. They'd need to uncover quite a lot of floor before they were able to judge whether there was a trapdoor or not. Who was to say that the man would put such an entrance right in the middle of the floor? It was much more likely to be tucked away in a corner, where there was little light.

'We're going to have to sweep them out completely,' he told the other three. 'If I know the old master, the trapdoor won't be where we expect it to be; it'll have been placed with great cunning.'

'Sometimes I wish my father had been just a little bit thicker, and this is one of them,' moaned Lady A, accepting her broom gloomily. 'When I went upstairs last night I thought we'd have our criminal behind bars by this morning. Now I'm not so sure we'll ever catch him.'

'I reckon we've got more chance than old Misery-Chops,' prophesied Enid, lighting a new cigarette from the butt of her old one.

'Come on, chop chop. Get a move on or we'll be here all day,' Beauchamp chided them, setting to work himself, and raising a great cloud of dust from the ancient straw, which made everybody sneeze. 'Come with me, Enid. I do believe we're going to need some buckets of water to dampen this lot down.'

The job still wasn't easy, even without the clouds of dust, and the two older members of the clearing crew needed to take frequent rests as their arthritic joints protested at such abuse.

'This is damned hard work,' protested Lady A.

'I've never done manual labour before,' complained Hugo.

'Well, this sort of job is hardly in my contract, and you don't even officially employ Enid yet,' Beauchamp reminded his employer.

At this reminder of her non-paid status, Enid downed her broom and took out her golden cardboard carton. 'If I'm not being paid, then you can hardly tell me off for slacking,' she said, a hint of mutiny in her voice.

'Enid, I do wish you'd give up that filthy habit. It makes you less than civil. In fact, sometimes, you're downright rude. This isn't the Enid Tweedie I've known and been friends with for donkey's years,' chastened Lady Amanda.

'I'll stop before the wedding,' she agreed, blushing slightly as the truth of this accusation hit home.

'Good. Bring the date forward if necessary. When is it to be, anyway?'

'The first Saturday in April. We'll need to get the dresses sorted out soon.'

'Oh, joy,' replied Lady A, who loved the honesty of a dress fitting the way she loved being prodded with red-hot pokers. 'I'll look forward to that, then.'

'Here we are,' called out Beauchamp, the ring of success in his voice. 'Right over here in this corner. I've found the ring and cleared the outline of the trapdoor. We should be able to open up and take a look down. Damn it! I didn't bring any torches with me. Will you get some Enid, and I'll get a spade.'

'What on earth do you need a spade for? The cellar's already been dug,' enquired Hugo.

'Because the trapdoor's probably firmly stuck down with old manure, and I'll no doubt need a spade to prise it open, after all this time.'

'Good thinking, my man.'

The ring was detachable, and Beauchamp could only think that it had been left in place either by accident or through arrogance. A lot depended on when it had last been opened.

It would appear that it had been used recently, as all the detritus round the edges of the trapdoor was loose, as if it had been sprinkled there to deceive, and the door itself opened easily without need of any use of the spade. The ladder beyond it had also been replaced with an aluminium one. Obviously the old wooden one had rotted into disuse over the decades.

'He's been here all right,' confirmed Beauchamp, descending and lighting one of the torches that Enid had fetched. As he swung the light around, he whistled and announced, 'It looks like it's all here, and so is Evergreen. What are we planning to do next? We had it all before, but lost it.'

'We'll have to take it all back to the house and lock it away. Or shall we just call the police?' Lady Amanda was having visions of them going backwards and forwards with wheelbarrows for hour upon hour.

'I think we ought to call the police. Inspector Moody would be exceedingly upset if we moved anything. We may obliterate fingerprints and destroy evidence,' added Beauchamp.

'Yes, it would be a bore, and quite a lot more hard work, if we moved it all,' said Hugo, whose eyes might need glasses for his newspaper, but were as sharp as needles when it came to sub-text.

'I'll tell you what I'll do.' Beauchamp had come to a decision. 'I'll take away the ladder and also remove the ring which pulls the trapdoor open. Then, if chummy returns,' – this still made Hugo turn his head, thinking he was being addressed – 'he'll not only know he's been rumbled, but will want to get the stuff away as quickly as possible.

'Well, that won't actually be a quick job, given the problem of the missing ring, then the missing ladder. We should have the boys in blue long before he's finished, and the cuffs clapped on him.' The manservant had it all worked out.

Unfortunately for him, Detective Inspector Moody was not feeling in a co-operative mood today. 'I don't think so, *Mr* Beecham. The last time you called me out, not only was it in the middle of the night, but it was also on a wild goose chase. If you think I'm coming out to that ruddy mausoleum again so quickly, you've got another think coming.

'If you want to entice me through those gates again, you'll have to have Jimmy the Jemmy Aldridge already caught and tied up. Not until then will I set foot on that woman's property again,' and he hung up.

The line went dead, leaving Beauchamp completely nonplussed, having been unable even to mention the status of the recently deceased Evergreen. Did the inspector mean what he'd said, or was he merely being facetious? The only thing to do was to take him at his word, and now he'd have to formulate a plan and go and apprise the other three of the new situation.

'That's exactly what he said,' he finished after his brief telling of the story.

'Bloody, bare-faced cheek of the man!' Lady Amanda was letting herself down while totally sober, today.

'But I've had time to think,' her manservant continued. 'I'm going to suggest that we start to remove the loot, starting with the stuff which can't be seen from the ladder, so it won't be visually missed, if he arrives while we're doing it.'

'But he'll see us.' This was the ever-cautious Hugo.

'Nonsense. There are plenty of old crates and boxes down here. There's lots of stuff we could hide in or behind.'

'If one is spry enough to move at that speed.' Hugo was still not convinced.

'There's no mains electricity down here. If you just froze, as you did as a child in musical statues, he simply wouldn't notice you, because you wouldn't be moving, and it's terribly gloomy down here.'

'But he'll have a torch.'

'Hugo, shut up! There are four of us. We've at least got a chance of ambushing and overpowering him.' Lady Amanda stepped in on Beauchamp's side to counteract her friend's negativity.

'What are you, a man or a mouse?' she asked.

And, although it was obviously a rhetorical question, he answered, 'Squeak!'

'Right, this is the end stable. If I open the boot room door, which is the one closest to the stable block for obvious reasons, we can take the stuff in through there, spending as little time out in open view as possible, so as not to be seen. We can take it through to a main room that locks, from there.' Beauchamp was in his element.

'We shall, in the meantime, need a bucket and some rope, so that things can be pulled up through the trapdoor. Then we'll need a couple of wheelbarrows to transport the stuff across to the house. It would be impossible – and disastrous with some stuff so fragile – to even attempt to do it by hand. Also, it would take too long.'

'Who's doing what, then?' Lady A wanted to get down to brass tacks, and just hoped he didn't expect her to lug wheelbarrows back and forth, to and from the house. She considered herself much too delicate a flower for that sort of activity. The sweeping had been bad enough, in her opinion.

'Hugo, I want you on bucket-loading duty down in the cellar.'

'Nice one, Beechy, old thing,' replied Hugo, uncharacteristically informally. He must have been very pleased with the task allotted to him.

'That's a bit of a cushy number, isn't it?' barked Lady A in annoyance.

'You, your ladyship, I want on bucket-hauling duty at the top, then tipping into wheelbarrow duty.'

'Fair enough.' That didn't sound too tough, although most of the stuff was a lot too delicate to be tipped, and would have to be carefully placed by hand.

'Enid and I will deal with the wheelbarrows. I shall wheel over to the house, where Enid will swap an empty barrow for a full one, then place the stuff in a room indoors. We'll be like a very posh chain gang, but without the actual chains.'

It was as Enid was placing her latest barrow-load of treasures and Beauchamp was just about to emerge from the boot room door, that he saw a figure insinuate itself very furtively through the stable door. Dear God! Was Jimmy the Jemmy back and about to burst in on Lady Amanda and Hugo?

He'd know there was someone down there, he now realised, simply because the trapdoor was open. With all speed, he rushed into the house to summon Enid, as an extra pair of hands against this devious and violent criminal.

Manda and Hugo were suddenly aware of shuffling noises above their heads, and dived down behind a small wall of discarded crates, which were probably waiting fruitlessly for another load of illegal booze that would now never arrive. Sure enough, they could hear the sound of somebody descending the ladder and making as little noise as possible.

Hugo began to shake, his knees visibly knocking. Lady Amanda signalled to him, in mime, that she was preparing to pounce on him – quite a sight. He nodded reluctantly, hoping that with the two of them, neither of whom was a lightweight, they could maybe knock him off balance. If they then shouted, they might be able to attract the attention of Beauchamp.

Beauchamp and Enid were, however, preparing to follow their quarry down the ladder. When the man got to the bottom, they shouted to him as they began to descend, and momentarily distracted him.

This was enough to give Lady A the signal that she had just struck lucky, and she launched herself from her hiding place, yelling as she pounced. Hugo followed suit, and all three figures landed on the floor in a heap, giving Beauchamp and Enid sufficient time to reach them, and help hold down their captive.

'Take off your trouser belt, please Mr Hugo,'

asked Beauchamp, not forgetting his manners in the excitement of the moment.

'Why?' Hugo was being dense; something at which he was a past master.

'Do you have any handcuffs about your person, sir?' asked the manservant.

There was silence for a few seconds, then, 'Oh! I see what you mean.'

Beauchamp used both his and Hugo's belts to secure Aldridge's wrists and ankles, while the combined weight of Lady A and Hugo held him firmly in place, face down, on the cellar floor. Finally, when he was unable to move a limb they flipped him on to his back.

'Good God! Turn him back again,' exclaimed Lady Amanda, and the other three echoed her.

'I shall have to telephone Detective Inspector Moody again and tell him that we have complied with his conditions,' said Beauchamp, heading for the ladder. 'I won't be able to get a signal down here.'

'What conditions?' his employer asked, in total ignorance of what Moody had said earlier.

'I'll tell you later, your ladyship. If you're going to have a conniption, I feel it will be more comfortable for you to do so in the house. Don't worry, I won't say a word,' and with this apparently cryptic sentence, he disappeared.

'Beauchamp! Hey, Beauchamp! Come back here this instant!'

Chapter Sixteen

At the police station, Inspector Moody was beginning to feel a little jittery about his dismissal of Beauchamp's information. Maybe he ought to have taken him seriously. The man would hardly phone him to tell him 'porky pies'. There must be something in what he said.

It was just about impossible that the whole thing might be a fabrication. He really ought to go out there and take a look – just to be on the safe side. It was better to be safe than sorry, after all.

He was just about to call Glenister, when the phone on his desk shrilled. It was that man again. 'You've what?' asked the detective in disbelief. 'Don't let him out of your sight and I'll be right out there.

'Glenister! Here! Now! That batty old cow and her cronies have only gone and caught our man. And they've recovered all the stolen goods and found the body, to boot. Get Spouph! We need to get over there half an hour ago.'

'Spouph's not here.'

'Why not? Where is he, then?'

'He said he was going out on the beat; left the station about an hour ago, said he'd be back at the end of his shift to get out of uniform.'

'Grab PC Baldwin, then. He'll do. He's a big strong lad who's capable of getting a dead body out of a cellar without too much trouble. Come on, man. Let's get going.'

The two men grabbed their outdoor coats, requisitioned Baldwin from behind the front desk, disturbing a very nice little read of the newspaper with his feet up for the duty desk sergeant, and sped off in Moody's car.

The inspector broke the speed limit the whole way to Belchester Towers, causing considerable wheel spin when he skidded to a halt at the front door. He was out of the car in a flash, and up the front steps, beginning immediately to pound on the front door in his eagerness for an arrest. This would be a feather in his cap, and no mistake.

It took some battering and a fair amount of yelling before anyone answered his frenzied summons, and it turned out to be Hugo who greeted him.

'Good afternoon, Inspector. How lovely to see you. I got Mrs Tweedie to give me a hand up the ladder, so that I could conduct you to where we have detained your man.'

'Tell me where he is, you silly old coot. I'll find him myself,' replied Moody, virtually foaming at the mouth in his eagerness to take his prisoner into custody.

'I think that's rather discourteous of you. Nevertheless, if you would care to follow me,' he replied, turning and setting off at a snail's pace down the hall.

'For the love of God, it'll take us a fortnight to get there if I follow you. Why won't you just give me directions, you long-winded old fool?'

Hugo stopped in his dreadfully slow tracks, looked over his shoulder and said, 'As we have taken the trouble to apprehend your criminal, the least you could is to show some courtesy, now you're here. I'll not take another step until you apologise for your extremely insulting comments.'

Moody couldn't believe either his eyes or his ears. Mr Triple-Barrelled had him by the short and curlies, and there wasn't a thing he could do about it. He had no idea where they had Aldridge incarcerated, and he knew exactly how long it took to search this property as his men had already done it, and that didn't include any of the outbuildings.

His teeth gritted together out of frustration, he finally ground out the words, 'I apologise for my bad manners. Take me to my prisoner.'

Hugo stared at him, turning right round to face him.

'Please,' Moody added, with a sickly grin. He'd be drawing his pension before he set eyes on Aldridge at this rate.

It seemed to take for ever, trailing along behind Hugo, but when they exited the main house through the door of the boot room, Moody realised that he had had no chance whatsoever of ever locating his man without this arthritic guide, as it seemed that Aldridge wasn't even in the main house, but in an outbuilding.

He noticed, with some puzzlement, the sea of straw, so old it was completely bleached of all colour, and the dried manure that seemed to adorn the yard outside the stables. The old boy was leading them towards the one on the end that had more of a pile outside than all of the others put together.

'You've not got him incarcerated in a stable, surely?' the inspector asked, in surprise. Surely it would have been easier and more convenient to have relocated him somewhere in the house, where the door could be locked to restrain him.

'Not quite, but you're getting warm,' replied Hugo in playful manner. 'Do you want another guess?'

'No! I want to frigging well get there, you geriatric old wreck.'

Hugo stopped dead again. 'Mind your mouth, or Manda will have your guts for garters. She won't be as lenient as me, as you well know, and she is a very good friend of the chief constable. I respectfully request that you button your lip, before we go any further.' Hugo was definitely getting huffy. It was turning into a very trying day.

With this threat in mind, Moody buttoned both of his lips together and followed on in complete silence, with the exception of a slight wheezing noise to his rear, which he failed to identify as Glenister and Baldwin venting their mirth at his discomfiture, as quietly as possible.

He spoke again as they entered the stable. 'Oh my God! He's not in a cellar, is he? I can't do ladders. Glenister, do something. I can't go down a ladder. It's a phobia I've suffered from since I was a child. Help me!'

'We'll get you down, sir,' Glenister assured him, patting him, in this sudden unexpected weakness, on the shoulder reassuringly. 'Baldwin and I will see you down, and back up again, in complete safety, won't we, Mike?'

'That we will,' PC Baldwin assured the inspector, his honest country face bearing a smile of complete confidence in his abilities.

Moody took a lot of help and coaxing to get down the ladder, even though it was a perfectly stable metal one, and not a worm-ridden, rotten wooden one that'd been there before, but he changed to a completely different man when he reached the bottom, turned around and opened his eyes, which he had closed tightly, in fear, during his descent.

'YES!' he yelled. 'THE BATTY OLD BIDDY'S ONLY GONE AND DONE IT!'

'I *beg* your pardon, Detective Inspector Moody?' enquired Lady Amanda in her most intimidating and withering tones, which were sharp enough to penetrate even this level of euphoria, and Moody gradually returned to the here and now.

'I'm sorry, your ladyship, but this is just so marvellous. You've got the stolen goods, although there don't seem to be as many of them as I'd have expected...'

'We were in the middle of transferring them into the house,' she interrupted, to explain.

'Jolly good show. And you've apprehended a very dangerous criminal. The day couldn't get any better. I don't even feel so bad about having to get up the ladder. Oh, and by gad, I've just noticed that you've located Evergreen's body, too. This is the perfect end to a dreadful spree of robbery and violence.'

None of those present had ever seen the man in such a happy mood; so complimentary and smiley that he seemed to be a changeling – could it be possible that there had really been a visitation to his home during the night? Absolutely not, concluded Beauchamp. He had been his usual obnoxious self on the phone earlier.

'Do you think you and your men could deal with taking in the prisoner, then return to clear out the rest of the loot and perhaps, move Evergreen to a more dignified resting place?' asked the manservant, eager to get his pair of pensioner heroes of the day away, and putting up their feet with some afternoon tea. He didn't want them overdoing things any more than they already had, then falling ill as a result, for he knew who would have to nurse them.

'Certainly, my man. Now, let's get the bugger turned over, if you'll all excuse my French,' said Moody, still beaming.

'De rien,' replied Lady A, Hugo and Beauchamp, in unison.

Even that didn't wipe the broad grin from the inspector's face, but his two colleagues, turning over the prisoner to reveal his face certainly did, for the colour bled from his face as from a red sock in a whites wash when he saw who had been captured.

'It looks awfully like...' He stuttered to a halt, unable to utter another word.

'That's because it is,' Lady Amanda almost crowed in triumph. 'You said I was wrong in The Clocky Hen. Actually, I was one hundred per cent right, and what fooled you was the lack of uniform, the coloured contact lenses to change the colour of the eyes, and the fake sideburns, which you evidently didn't even notice. I was right all along, and you didn't even recognise one of your own officers with whom you had been closely working. My house-point, I believe, Inspector.

'Do allow me to introduce you to Jimmy "the Jemmy" Aldridge, aka PC Spouph. You should have guessed from that name that there was 'summat' afoot. Spouph indeed! What have *you* been smoking? The man's obviously a dab hand at forging paperwork.

'I don't know where you think you get off telling me I can't identify a man who's actually been in my own house. And as for you, I think you should pay a visit to a well-known chain of opticians for some spectacles. You obviously need them.'

'Dear God! Spouph even had the cheek to case out the joint before the robberies, when he was in uniform,' gasped Moody in disbelief, blushing at what a blind idiot he'd been. He then remembered what he had said earlier in the case, pulled the sides of his eyes, so that they became slits, and uttered, 'Ying tong, ying tong.' He hadn't got one over on the old bag after all.

'Sorry, guv,' said Spouph/Aldridge from the cellar floor. 'It seemed foolproof. But I'm not putting up my hands to them maids. They was nothin' to do with me and I'll not go down for them.'

'Tell that to the Marines,' Moody advised him.

'No, honestly, guv. They was nothin' to do with me.'

'Come along you two. When these good people have left, I want you, Glenister, to help me up the ladder – I'm not so bad going up – and you, Baldwin, to see if you can get Evergreen in a fireman's lift and follow suit. Then you can both come back down to get this villain up, and carry him to the car. I'm not taking those restraints off him until he's safely behind bars.'

The heroic four re-entered the house via the boot room door, which had not seen so much action since a much younger Lady A and her parents had hosted the local hunt, her father being MFH (Master of Fox Hounds) at the time, when the stables had been in constant use.

When Amanda passed into the room where Enid had laid out all the stolen valuables that had been successfully returned to the house, she stopped dead and put her hands up to her mouth.

'I know it looks a bit like a car boot sale,' admitted Enid, 'but we'll soon get everything back where it belongs don't you worry about it.'

'It looks just like an antique shop,' said Lady Amanda in hushed tones of enchantment. Hugo's brow furrowed with trepidation, and he found he was holding his breath.

'That's what I want to do,' Lady A declared. 'I don't want to go back to doing tours of the house. That would never have worked, and look what happened when we tried it! I want to open an antique shop in one of the disused rooms here.

'I can sort out all the stuff I really dislike, and we can do cups of tea and coffee, and have a little tea shop in the room next door. It'll be an absolute joy, and I'll feel that I'm doing something useful. There are hardly any antique shops in Belchester, and I can pester the council to put up a sign in the town, to point people in our direction, and we can advertise, too.

'You see to interviewing for a new head

groundsman, Beauchamp, and, while you're at it, see about some new maids and general gardeners. I'm going to start going through the rooms to gather stock, once this lot is all put away, and ordering some tablecloths – no, strike that. I bet we've got tons of them in the various presses around the house.

'The same goes for tea sets, pots, and spoons. I'll bet there are cupboards just bursting with useful stuff. We shouldn't have to spend a penny to get things going. Hurray! Life's going to be so exciting. We'll open after the honeymoon.'

'I'm going outside for a fag,' said Enid with a dismissive sneer.

'And I'm going to buy you some patches and wean you off that dreadful, mood-altering drug,' muttered Beauchamp.

Chapter Seventeen

Later

It was several days later that Moody did them the courtesy to come up to the house with Glenister to take their statements. He didn't want those four coming down to the station and ragging him about what a fool he'd been, as he'd sworn Glenister and Baldwin to secrecy about his little misidentification in The Clocky Hen.

'Hello, Inspector,' called Hugo as he espied the detective coming down the hall. 'We've been ragging Manda by calling her "Eagle-Eye", saying it's her tribal name, ever since we apprehended that villain.'

'Really? How jolly for you all,' replied Moody, looking flustered. 'I wonder if you could spare me a few minutes of your time – all four of you – to give your accounts of your involvement in the case that you so thoroughly wrapped up the other week?'

'No problem,' sounded Lady A's voice from the drawing room. 'Come on in and sit down.'

When they had all complied with Moody's wishes, he said, preparatory to leaving, 'You know what that Aldridge said when you had him trussed up in the stable cellar? That he hadn't done those women?'

'Yes,' they all four agreed.

'Well, he's sticking to that absolutely firmly. He's quite happy to admit that he killed Mangel and Evergreen – the forensics department has got him bang-to-rights on both of those – but he's adamant that he never touched the maids.'

'And has the forensics department not got him bang-to-rights on those other two as well?' asked Lady A, interested in what sounded like a bizarre little problem, given what the man didn't seem to mind holding up his hands for.

'No. It's really weird, but they haven't found any forensic evidence at all to indicate who killed them, so we can't charge him.'

'He'll go down for a good long stretch for the two men and the robberies, though,' chimed in Glenister, 'so it's not of vital importance that we nail him for the two women. We've got plenty on him as it is.'

The Next Day

Enid had arranged for Lady Amanda and her to go dress-hunting. She'd decided against having a rather middle-aged and non-fussy dress, thinking that, the last time she got married, she and her first husband had had almost no money, and she had borrowed a dress.

This time Beauchamp said she could have whatever she wanted, price no object, and she knew he meant it, for she had seen his bank statement when he'd accidentally left it out on display on his desk top for a few minutes, recently.

They headed for Belchester, which was just the right sort of town to boast three separate wedding shops, Enid determined that they should not return before the shops closed. She wanted her time in the spotlight, and Lady A could only comply with her wishes, whether she liked it or not. This was to be HER day, and nothing would spoil it.

The first shop that Enid insisted they headed for was Bridal Dreamz in North Street. Enid nearly swooned with delight when she saw the rows and rows of pale, floaty meringues. Lady Amanda, on the other hand, wondered if Enid had taken her into a shop for hot air balloons by mistake.

'You'll never get me up in one of those,' she muttered, out of her friend's hearing, while Enid drifted along, her eyes like saucers, as she surveyed the sort of thing she had never had reason – or funds – to be able to look at before in her life.

Very carefully, she selected an ivory confection large enough to hide almost an entire bridal party in its nets and layers. Putting that aside, she moved to bridesmaids' dresses and began her mesmerised drift again, finally drawing to a halt in front of a pink froth that made Lady A wince, she watched her take it from the rail.

Then she chided herself. Enid hadn't had much of a life, when one considered it. Her husband had been a pretty poor specimen who couldn't provide anything better than one of the crumbling cottages in Plague Alley. He had shuffled off his mortal coil pretty swiftly, only for her demanding old mother to move in with her 'just for the company'.

She had spent years in and out of hospital for fairly trivial matters, almost as a means of self-defence, Lady A thought. Now she had Beauchamp, and was going to live in the big house. She deserved her time as star of the show, and it was only for a few hours of one day. She'd comply without a fight. Enid deserved it for all the things she had helped her with and done for her over the years.

With her head bowed to hide the look of dismay and despair on her face, Manda held out a hand to take the frothy confection of lace and frills and headed towards the changing rooms, dismissing the help of an assistant, as she was perfectly capable of dressing herself, thank you very much.

Enid happily paired up with an assistant and headed for a changing room with a sign that proudly announced that it was the 'Brides' Transformation Suite', with professional aid in the difficulties of putting on such a complicated garment.

Enid emerged long before there was any movement from the other changing room, and stood admiring herself in a full-length mirror. Really, she did look like a princess, if one disregarded the age of the face at the top of the concoction. Still, plenty of women were renewing their vows these days, probably just to get the chance to wear the sort of dress they couldn't afford first time round, so she would hardly stand out as unique.

The curtains of the changing room that housed the maid-of-honour-to-be moved violently, and a low sort of growling noise began to issue from inside the cubicle. When Enid became aware of it, she stood her ground. She didn't want to interfere, if her friend were at a delicate stage of the proceedings; maybe in an embarrassing stage of undress.

The growling grew louder and became interspersed with little grunting noises, which rose to a crescendo and ended with a positive howl of rage and despair and a monster issued back into the body of the shop.

It had short, fat legs which were working like pistons to propel it forward. From where the knees would be to above the top, was just a positive blancmange of pinkness, layers of delicate lace trailing in its wake like tentacles. It only stopped careering along and moaning when it collided with a sturdy pillar clad in mirrors, coming to a halt with a sigh like a steam train.

'Amanda?' enquired Enid, tentatively, although who else could it be? She had only just got used to dropping the Lady, as her friend had insisted she do since she and Beauchamp had become betrothed.

'Grrrr, hrhlmph, ahhhhhgh!' declared the devoured customer.

'I'll just get an assistant to help us, and you'll be out in a jiffy.' Even as Enid went in search of aid, she realised that, in the dress, she was gliding, not merely walking.

She returned, pretty sharpish, with one of the shop's employees, who feared for the safety of her stock. The apparition was now bending at what was probably the waist, and bowing up and down. An arm suddenly appeared through the material at the top, and the shop assistant moved in to intervene, before the inhabitant of the dress reduced it to unsaleable rags.

'Do allow me to assist you, madam,' she carolled, in anxious tones.

'Grrr, wossit umpher elph,' came from inside the giant fondant fancy.

The assistant suddenly seemed to be all arms, and in only a couple of minutes, she had straightened out the dress, tamed it, and got it properly fitted on to its incandescent occupant.

'There, madam. I think you'll find that satisfactory. Would madam care to take a look in our mirrors, so that she can see it from all angles?'

'Blasted thing positively ate me,' puffed Lady A. 'If you hadn't intervened, I swear it was just about to start to digest me. Oh, bloody Norah! What, in the name of all that's holy do I look like? I'm tricked out like a giant cake. Whatever will Hugo say? He'll become incontinent with laughter. I'll never live this down.'

A very quiet voice behind her almost whispered, 'I like it,' and reality returned. It was to be

Enid's day. She mustn't be so selfish or rebellious as to spoil anything for her.

'Do you like it, Enid? Let me take a look at you. My goodness, you're transformed. Beauchamp will want to ravish you as soon as he sets eyes on you,' she said, as generously as possible, hoping that no one mistook *her* for the wedding cake and tried to cut a slice out of her, for she now knew that she'd be wearing this mountain of pink icing on the day.

'Don't you like it, Amanda?' asked Enid, with a catch in her voice, as if she feared perfection was to be snatched from her when she had only just caught sight of it.

'If it's what you would like me to wear for your wedding, then it must be perfect,' said Lady A unexpectedly, both hands behind her back with all her fingers crossed at the blatant lie. 'And you look like a million dollars.'

'Oh, thank you so much. Er, what actually happened in the changing cubicle?'

'It would appear that I got some of the hooks that attach pieces of the froth to the right part of the dress entangled with my hair grips and, the more I struggled, the worse things got. All over now, though. Let's get into our own clothes and get these ready to be delivered, unless you'd like to leave them here until nearer the wedding.'

'They'll have to be altered anyway,' replied Enid, knowingly. 'They're all made with the hem unsewn, so that there's no problem with extra-tall women. We'll have to come in for a proper fitting before the wedding for the length, then we can take them away.'

'How knowledgeable of you, dear. I just thought it was the current fashion, to have the garment about two feet too long.'

'You're not very tall, are you? – no offence meant. That's why there was so much spare.'

'Good things come in little packages,' concluded Lady A.

'And so does poison,' mouthed Enid, who was longing for a puff on one of her filter-tipped, king-sized drug-sticks.

Chapter Eighteen

That Evening

After Beauchamp had put away the Rolls and entered the house, Lady Amanda, who was still in the hall, clapped her hands in the air, as if preparatory to breaking out into a fit of flamenco, and cried, 'Come along, my man. I shall have a Bridesmaid Cooler. It's definitely cocktail time, or at least a quarter to it, and I deserve something with a bit of a kick and just the right name, after what I've been through.'

'Did everything go all right?' he asked, genuinely interested, for he could not see his employer putting up with a lot of trailing round bridal shops.

'It was perfect heaven,' replied Enid, with an uncharacteristically dreamy look on her face. 'We only had to go into one shop, and we found both my dress and Amanda's.'

'How spiffing,' he replied, letting out his breath like a spurt of steam, in relief. He'd been nurturing a mental image of Enid arriving back in tears, with Lady Amanda spitting fire, after a fruitless trip round every bridal shop in the city. 'I'll prepare a Bridesmaid Cooler for you, your ladyship.'

'I'll have the same, I think,' Enid declared. 'I may not be a bridesmaid, but I definitely need a bit of a cooler, after fighting my way in and out of that complicated wedding dress.'

'I shall wear a morning suit – with top hat, I think.'

'Perfect!'

'Chop chop, Beauchamp. I shall die of thirst if you don't get a wiggle on. I've got a hard day ahead of me tomorrow, with heaven knows how many builders to phone about converting your flat.'

'How exciting life has become. I don't think I've ever been so happy.'

'Oh, we'll soon fix that,' said Lady A, but she had a twinkle in her eye, to show she was only joking.

After a fairly early evening meal that day, where the talk had been almost exclusively about the wedding, Lady Amanda reminded them that she'd be contacting several builders in the morning, to arrange for estimates for the conversion of some of the rooms into a self-contained flat for them.

'And I shall need to go home early this evening,' Enid informed them. 'If I'm going to be living here, I shall have to start doing something with my own little house.'

'Are you going to rent it out for income, or sell

it?' asked Lady A.

'I haven't quite made up my mind. I think I'll probably put it up for rent; that way my mother can't land on me again, and I can put it on the market when I've got used to the idea. If she claims she needs somewhere to go, when she falls out with my sister, she can camp out there if I haven't got a tenant. I don't ever want to be in the situation where she thinks she can muscle her way in on our home here.'

'Heaven forbid! I should never allow it.'

'Get in the queue,' replied Enid vehemently. 'Whatever I do, I need to clear out everything that is surplus to needs, and start transferring some of my stuff up here. I'll definitely need a skip before I've finished. There's shedloads of stuff in the attic, and every nook and cranny is full of unnecessary ornaments and souvenirs – stuff like that I just don't need now I've got a completely new life beckoning.'

Beauchamp positively preened at this last statement, but it wasn't just he that had transformed her existence: it was the detecting, and the increased closeness of the friendship she had with Lady A. Everything had changed since she had first gone 'undercover', just after Mr Hugo had moved in. She had never felt so alive.

'Come along,' said Beauchamp, 'and I'll get the Rolls out again. We can have a singsong in the car on the way home.'

'Scrumptious,' replied Enid.

Lady A turned her face away, so that she could make a 'being sick' face without being observed.

Enid entered her little house in Plague Alley feeling rather nostalgic. She might not have led the high life under its rather wavy roof, but she had spent a great number of years in its shelter.

She and her first husband, Ted, had moved there shortly after they had married; they had both been so young. Her Ted was not the sharpest knife in the canteen, when closely examined – she supposed he was more akin to a spoon – but they had survived.

They had just never prospered, and Ted had spent a lot of time out of work. Many of the years they had lived there, she had been the sole breadwinner. In fact, she didn't really want to think about Ted any more. Better to leave the memories undisturbed. No point in raking up the past when the future was out there waiting for her.

Their only child had been their poor stillborn son. Enid knew she could never withstand that heartbreak again, when she had looked at his little body so perfect, so beautiful, lacking only one thing – that essential spark of life. She had thought she would die of grief and join him, for a long time after his poor little body was buried. No, she *must* not think of the past.

She wandered around, picking up little ornaments and framed photos that reminded her of happier times. She had come here as a young bride. She was leaving it as a grey-haired woman. Somehow, though, she felt the best years were still before her. Beauchamp was a one-off, the like of which she never thought she would meet, and here she was preparing to marry him. How lucky she was.

She'd start with her wardrobe, she decided, beginning to mount the stairs. There were a lot of drab garments in the various cupboards and drawers on the first floor that she simply could not bear to wear again. She needed some new clothes that just sang with colour, the way her life was beginning to. They didn't have to be expensive; just loud.

She knew she was wasting a lot of money on cigarettes at the moment, and made the sudden decision to give up, and put what she had been spending on this highly addictive weed into a clothes fund. She'd buy everything just a bit loose, as she was bound to put on a bit of weight when she didn't have this appetite suppressant any more, and was a married woman, much more content with her lot.

The decision brought a big smile to her face, as she hurled grey skirts, beige cardigans, and brown jumpers into a big heap in the middle of her bedroom floor. She'd have to go downstairs and get some black bags to put them in. She'd even take them to the charity shop. It wasn't that they were particularly worn; just that she was a different person now, and didn't want to be seen in such drab colours.

Underwear; she'd need complete new underwear, especially drawers, for she didn't want her new husband to see her in the twice round the gasworks' numbers she currently wore. She'd just have to keep a few pairs back so that she had time to get to the shops.

Before she knew it, she had filled three big bags, and it was past midnight. She'd have to get to bed, as her fiancé would be calling for her in not too many hours. She'd spend the next couple of weeks coming here in the evenings, sorting things out into keep, take and discard categories.

She'd probably have to take some boxes with her to sort at her leisure: those that involved memories, and needed more careful consideration. She actually had the opportunity to edit her past, should she so wish.

They could use the trailer and take things to the tip, or really push out the boat and order a giant skip to take everything, once it was sorted, for no way was she going to leave it out in the street overnight so that her neighbours could fill it with old mattresses and rusty fridges. She'd talk to her husband-to-be about it, and at this thought, a shiver of excitement at what the future might hold shook her body.

When Beauchamp returned, he cleared away everything from dinner and put on the dishwasher. He then took care of his late evening duties so that they were out of the way. His last task, before having some time to himself, was to make two cups of cocoa so that Lady Amanda and Hugo could take them up to bed to sip while they had a little read of their library books.

When he had seen them safely up the stairs, he locked up, retired to his pantry, which was sacrosanct, then shook and strained himself a double Wolf's Lair, before sinking down into the ancient armchair he kept in his sanctuary of sanctuaries for cogitating. He'd had a lot on his mind lately, and he felt the need for a deep think.

Of course he regretted what he had done. Who wouldn't? But he knew there was no way he could have avoided it, and there was always a way to put it right without too much inconvenience. He had realised the first time it had happened, that it was part and parcel of who he was, and he could no more change that, than he could lasso the moon for his bride-to-be.

It had been building up inside him for a long time, just as it had before, and he had to control it until he could unleash it without anyone he cared for being caught up in it. After all, no one would ever know. And given the spacing between the two attacks, he would probably be dead before it happened again, which was a good thing.

It was only *he,* however, who knew who had killed those two occasional maids, and only *he* that knew why Jimmy 'the Jemmy' Aldridge would never confess to their murders. It hadn't, after all, been him who had committed them. The man was as totally innocent of these crimes as he was of the gunpowder plot and the great train robbery.

Of course, he regretted that he had had to ... do them in, he supposed, was the kindest way of putting it. It had to be someone, just as it had to be someone before, and they would be the least missed. They weren't inextricably bound up with the day-to-day working of the household, both were getting on a bit, and neither had large families, let alone very satisfying existences. Also, they were a couple of nosy old bags to boot, and he couldn't risk them going through his desk or anything underhand like that. It could have proved disastrous.

Actually, he felt rather smug about his creativity with these two executions. Florrie Searle's demise from the blows from the A flat clarinet had caused him particular glee. Firstly, he had remembered to use his footman's gloves when carrying out this murder, and he had used this particular instrument just for pure badness's sake – he knew how his mistress loved it. And his victim had suspected nothing, as it was only the butler who was in the room while she was working.

Edie Hare's death had been carried out in a most ingenious way, in his opinion. When he'd heard her going outside to get her bicycle, he'd rushed into the domestic quarters. There was just enough time for him to get a leg of lamb from the freezer.

With this hidden behind his back, he had gone outside on the pretext that he thought she might have left her gloves on the hall table. When she had turned away to get off the machine she was just mounting, he had bopped her over the head and roughly concealed the body in the shrubbery. Then he had merely washed the blood from the joint of meat, and put it in the refrigerator for use during the next few days. No forensic evidence existed of either crime.

At least this time he knew what was happening inside his head. The last time – the first – he had been terrified of what he was thinking, and the safest way to let out the pressure – blow down the boilers, as he thought of it – was to nick the brake pipes on the master's car. As luck would have it, with the amount of alcohol the old master had consumed, the chances were very high that they would have gone off the road anyway, and been killed without any contribution from him.

He had been distraught when he realised that his own mother was in the car alongside the master, but he learned to live with his guilt and settle back into his normal routine as though nothing had happened. And as his mother had felt no guilt about having sex with the old master and actually bearing his child, so Beauchamp felt no guilt – more a passing sadness – at the deaths he had caused recently. They were necessary for him to clear his mind, so that he didn't lose it.

He'd be perfectly all right now, for at least a couple of decades. If it happened again in the future, he'd find a 'safe' way of dealing with it, as he had this time. His little aberration didn't make him mad, just different, in his eyes. And, if he was careful, no one'd ever know about it, save himself.

He rose to his feet, feeling much more calm and contented, now that he'd had this little rationalisation with himself, moved to the cocktail ingredients, and stirred and strained an 'Incredible Cocktail'. He felt he deserved it.

Chapter Nineteen

Some Days Later

Beauchamp had had the good sense to provide both ladies – in the interests of subduing Lady Amanda – with a double tulip glass apiece, filled with an extra-large serving of a Hen Night

Zipper-Ripper – although he did not divulge the name of the drink, lest he scandalise them – before he drove them to the dress fitting session. At least, with some alcohol down her throat, his employer was liable to be a good bit nicer than she would be stone cold sober.

The Day Before the Wedding

The cake was delivered on the Friday afternoon. It was a traditional, white wedding cake with five tiers and icing flowers and lace. On the top was a (plastic) model of a bride and groom and, although it was nothing out of the way, the mere sight of it made Enid shiver with secret delight at what was to come in the very near future.

The night before the wedding was not treated as a traditional hen or stag night. They were simply too old for those sort of shenanigans. Instead, Lady Amanda arranged with caterers to serve them a meal consisting of lobster bisque, beef wellington, and baked Alaska. They were three dishes all four of them were very fond of, and she raided the out-of-bounds bit of the cellar for some vintage champagne the market price of which she dared not even imagine.

Before the meal arrived, Beauchamp provided them all with some more Hen Night Zipper-Rippers, this time telling them the name when he served them, which produced a disapproving frown at this stage of the evening, but much hilarity, later on, when it was recalled after a good bellyful of alcohol.

After they had eaten, he and Hugo retired to his pantry and each enjoyed a pint of Old Speckled Hen, and had a bit of a chinwag. It was all very low key and relaxed, as it was back in the drawing room, where Enid and Lady Amanda enjoyed an almost last chat before Enid became Mrs Beauchamp.

Nothing outrageous occurred, and no one went to bed really befuddled. Things boded well for the morrow.

The Wedding Day

The day of the wedding itself dawned bright and sunny, with even a bit of warmth in the air, to herald the arrival of spring. Lady Amanda had booked the caterers, her treat, and they arrived shortly after sun-up to prepare the rooms that were going to be used.

They had decided not to hire a chauffeur, dispensing with the tradition that the groom arrived at the church first. It had been arranged that professionals would have arrived to help both women into their complicated dresses – Enid's with veil and bouquet – deal with their hair and make-up (also courtesy of Lady A), and they would all leave the big house in the same car, arriving at the church together, although the groom and best man would take their places in the right-hand front row before the bride and maid-of-honour got out of the car.

Hugo was as proud as Punch to have been asked to give her away, and positively over the moon with his kilt, which arrived on time, complete with sporran and the rest of the rigout. Lady A decided that even she would allow her hair to be done and her face and nails painted, for this very special day in the life of her chief undercover agent, and everything looked set fair for the rest of the proceedings.

When they were all suitably primped and attired, they would all go in the Rolls together to arrive as the bridal 'mob', rather than party, at the church of St Michael-in-the-Fields, which was actually on West Street, and should ensure that there was a good crowd to ogle the bride on her special day, as she went inside to receive her new matrimonial chains – invisible, of course.

Beauchamp had even arranged that both women be served with champagne while they were got ready, so that neither of them would be in a state of panic; mellow, rather, and relaxed enough to enjoy the occasion. He had even arranged – at great expense, although only he knew this – to have a videographer film the day for posterity and their future enjoyment.

The ceremony was to be at two o'clock, so everyone had fitted in a snack – nothing that could spoil their appearance, and had worn bibs while they ate – and the wedding party congregated in the hall of The Towers at one-thirty. Enid could not claim the bride's prerogative of arriving late, because they were all going together, and the vicar was likely to have a heart attack, so old and frail was he, if he thought that none of the stars of the show were going to turn up.

It took longer than they had thought to load

such full dresses into the back of the Rolls, and Hugo was quite out of breath when he finally took his place in the passenger seat. Beauchamp had just turned the ignition key, when Enid screeched, 'My bouquet! I've left it on a table in the hall,' and Beauchamp rushed back into the house to get it, finding the posy that Lady Amanda was to carry, abandoned carelessly beside it. Golly, that was a close one!

The car drew up outside St Michael-in-the-Fields at one-forty-five precisely. Beauchamp had driven deliberately slowly, not only to gauge the timing perfectly, but so that his fiancée in the back seat should have as long as possible to enjoy her experience of going to the church in all her finery.

The vicar was already waiting outside for them and, at this signal that there was to be a wedding this afternoon, as the bells were ringing as well, to indicate that it was not a funeral, quite a crowd had gathered to see the bride arrive.

This was most gratifying for Enid, but mortifying for Lady Amanda, who fervently hoped that none of her friends or acquaintances was lurking in its depths. She couldn't bear the thought that she should be seen by one of them when she was dressed as a strawberry trifle. She'd never live it down.

It was even more of a kerfuffle getting the two ladies out from the back of the car than it had been getting them in. Installing them had been a job mainly of stuffing the plethora of layers into the car and getting the doors shut without trapping, and thus marking, any of them.

Getting them out was another matter entirely, as it involved straightening out said multiple layers, and straightening them into a semblance of what the designer had intended when he had drawn his sketches.

At one point, Lady A managed almost to do a somersault, and, at another, she pointed out that, somehow, she seemed to have several layers of lacy stuff tucked into her knickers but, eventually, they were ready, Beauchamp beetled off, and the other three got into the correct order to process down the aisle.

Enid beamed from behind her veil on Hugo's arm, and Lady Amanda blushed furiously as a familiar voice called from the crowd, 'Hey, Manda, didn't recognise you for a moment. Nice threads.' She couldn't immediately put a name to the voice, but it would all come out in good time, having been passed round her whole crowd of friends, and she'd get dreadfully ragged for it.

Dammit all, it was Enid's day, and there'd be a picture of the bridal party in next week's Belchester and the County newspapers. But what the hell! Enid had been a staunch friend and a willing helper for years. She owed it to her.

They processed, not to the usual bridal march, but to Parry's 'I Was Glad', which was such a joyous piece of music, and a little more suitable for a lady of Enid's vintage. The choir, swelled to a full complement, as befitting the pedigree of the bridal party, sang along lustily, giving it all they had got, and Lady A swelled with pride, quite unexpectedly.

Hugo handed Enid over to Beauchamp when

they reached the front of the church, the man-servant gently lifting and replacing her veil to the back of her head, and Lady A took her bouquet of red roses, to hold along with her much smaller but just as beautiful posy of freesias. Both of them turned towards the vicar, and the service began.

There was a minor sensation during the 'Do you take this...' section, when Beauchamp's fore-names were revealed. Certainly, Lady Amanda had no clue what he had been christened and, apparently, neither did Enid or anyone else. When the vicar enunciated 'Jean-Marie Michel' in his frightfully English accent, not only did he receive a frightful glower from the groom, but a titter of amusement which filled the church, temporarily halting the ceremony, and both bride and groom blushed to the roots of their hair.

The church was exquisitely decorated, and candles had been lit, at Beauchamp's special request, to create an extra-romantic mood. The vicar had just reached the point where he asked if anyone here present knew of any just cause or impediment why these two should not be joined in holy matrimony, when someone at the back cleared their throat loudly and purposefully...

THE END, for now...

COCKTAIL RECIPES

BRIDESMAID COOLER

2 measures gin
1 measure lemon juice
½ measure sugar syrup
1 dash Angostura bitters
4 measures ginger ale
Add to a glass filled with ice

CRATER FACE

1½ measures Madeira
1 measure bourbon
1 teaspoon crème de banana
1 teaspoon grenadine
Add to a glass 3/4-filled with broken ice

HAMMER HORROR

1 measure vodka
1 measure Kahlua
4 tablespoons vanilla ice-cream
Blend briefly and sprinkle with grated chocolate before adding straws

HEART THROB

½ measure Kahlua
½ measure whipping cream
¾ measure dark rum

Pour in layers over a spoon into a tall narrow glass

HELL FROZEN OVER

1 measure sloe gin
1 measure Canadian whisky
⅓ measure lemon juice
1 measure lemonade
Add to a glass ½-filled with broken ice and garnish with slice of kiwi fruit and a cherry.

HEN NIGHT ZIPPER-RIPPER

½ measure white rum
1 measure advocaat
¾ measure mandarin juice
¾ measure lime juice
¼ measure grenadine
Shake and strain and garnish with a slice of lime and a cherry.

INCREDIBLE COCKTAIL

1½ measures Canadian whisky
½ measure Glayva
¼ measure Punt e Mes
Shake with broken ice and serve unstrained.

JUG WOBBLER

1 measure gin
1 measure apple schnapps
1 measure dry vermouth
¼ measure Pernod
4 measures 7-Up
Serve in an ice-filled glass.

LAUGH A MINUTE

1 measure cherry brandy
1 measure vermouth rosso
½ measure amaretto
2 measures lemonade
Shake and strain over ice before adding lemonade.

LAWNMOWER

1 measure bison grass vodka (as if!)
1 teaspoon sweet sherry
3 measures lemonade
Serve in a full glass of broken ice.

OLD MOORHEN'S SHREDDED SPORRAN

1 measure scotch
½ measure Drambuie
½ measure Mandarine Napoleon
1 teaspoon parfait amour
2 measures pineapple juice
1 measure guava nectar
¼ measure lemon juice
1 teaspoon almond syrup
Shake briefly with crushed ice, and garnish with a slice of lemon, a cherry and straws.

VIRGIN MARY

5 measures tomato juice
½ teaspoon lemon juice
2 dashes Worcestershire sauce
4 drops Tabasco sauce
1 pinch celery salt
1 small pinch black pepper

Shake and strain, then garnish with a celery stick.
(Note: this is just a Bloody Mary without the vodka, and would only have been tomato juice and Worcester sauce in the pub where Lady A ordered two.

WOLF'S LAIR
1 measure brandy
1 measure peach schnapps
½ measure Barenfang
1 measure whipping cream
Shake and strain.

HAPPY – HIC – COCKTAIL TIME!

The publishers hope that this book has given you enjoyable reading. Large Print Books are especially designed to be as easy to see and hold as possible. If you wish a complete list of our books please ask at your local library or write directly to:

Magna Large Print Books
Magna House, Long Preston,
Skipton, North Yorkshire.
BD23 4ND

This Large Print Book for the partially sighted, who cannot read normal print, is published under the auspices of

THE ULVERSCROFT FOUNDATION

THE ULVERSCROFT FOUNDATION

... we hope that you have enjoyed this Large Print Book. Please think for a moment about those people who have worse eyesight problems than you ... and are unable to even read or enjoy Large Print, without great difficulty.

You can help them by sending a donation, large or small to:

The Ulverscroft Foundation,
1, The Green, Bradgate Road,
Anstey, Leicestershire, LE7 7FU,
England.

or request a copy of our brochure for more details.

The Foundation will use all your help to assist those people who are handicapped by various sight problems and need special attention.

Thank you very much for your help.